NATHANIEL'S TREASURE

SHERI LYNN

Published by Blushing Books
An Imprint of
ABCD Graphics and Design, Inc.
A Virginia Corporation
977 Seminole Trail #233
Charlottesville, VA 22901

Sheri Lynn
Nathaniel's Treasure

EBook ISBN: 978-1-64563-525-3
Print ISBN: 978-1-64563-526-0
Audio ISBN: 978-1-64563-527-7
v2

Chapter 1

Thousands of pirates were active between 1650 and 1720, and these years are sometimes known as the 'Golden Age' of piracy.

Standing on land again felt incredible. Though Priscilla had no regrets regarding her decision to sneak onto the ship captained by her father, she missed the ground beneath her feet every day. They had been sailing almost two weeks, and even though they stopped in Nassau, she couldn't persuade him to let her leave the ship. Finally, today, he agreed. Though after many tears and pleas.

A small twinge of remorse entered her thoughts. She knew he had to deal with her mother eventually. No one wanted that. The tongue lashing surely waiting for him when he returned home sent shivers down her spine. Her mother would berate and blame him for Priscilla's defiance to her every move. She couldn't remember a time her mother didn't deride him for spoiling her too much and for encouraging her adventurous spirit.

No one knew she had no plans to return. She hated Charles Town. She hated that life. Her days consisted of wearing uncomfortable clothing, answering the boring gentleman callers her mother paraded before her, followed by tense dinners consisting of arguments and pressure for her to behave as an officer's daughter and to marry.

If her mother could see her now, she would probably faint. The steady ripples of the ocean waves washed up on her feet, kissing her ankles. Finn, the escort her father sent with her, sat just inside a patch of sparse greenery, his back to her. Her father gave strict instructions. Finn mustn't take her near the docks and remain as inconspicuous as possible.

Finding this vacant beach adhered to all that, and being alone, she removed all her clothing except her shift. She twirled and skipped along the shoreline. The freedom she experienced in those few moments, made all the lies she told worth it. She cried and prayed for forgiveness each night. Each day it became more and more difficult to meet her father's eyes. It entered her mind to use the opportunity he gave her that day to part ways with him. But she couldn't bring herself to do it. She never wished to cause him any worry and heartache. Perhaps she should write him a letter when the time came. Maybe the thought of leaving him and all she knew behind frightened her and she had yet to admit it.

And, she hated deceiving Gideon, the only suitor who did make her body tingle, in even her most private parts. Agreeing to accept his proposal after she returned was the only way to procure his assistance in getting her on the ship. Rumors of his sexual prowess circulated among the ladies. She had no doubt he would move on. A fanatical flirt, she couldn't imagine him ever being faithful to one woman. And that fact didn't bother her. She never planned to marry him.

Gathering a few more shells, she looked back to Finn. Next

to Finn's slumped forward body, a wild man stood and stared directly at her. She didn't know what to do. Check on Finn? Call for help? Run?

It didn't look like the wild one had a weapon drawn. He did have a huge sword hanging from his side, and a pistol on the other. The breeze blew his long brown hair across his sun-darkened face. Gold and gems glinted from his ears, wrists and hands when they caught the sunlight. Never had she known of a man wearing such adornments. He started towards her. She darted off down the beach.

A few strides in, an arm wrapped around her middle, lifting her off her feet. The air left her lungs; she couldn't draw in a breath to scream.

"Where ya think you running off to, Angel? I saw you. I want you. I'll take you." He tightened his right arm around her, and using the other, fisted her hair, forcing her to look into his golden eyes. They were the lightest brown she ever saw, like the sunset over the open sea. "You like what you see, Miss?" he asked, in a deep, intimidating voice.

As shocking as it was, she did. His shirt lay open baring his chest. She didn't know if it lacked ties, or if he chose to wear it that way. He had a small patch of dark hair just above the waist of his trousers. Improper or not, she didn't avert her gaze. She wondered if it continued lower.

He tossed her over his shoulder and sauntered off away from the beach, toting her like a sack of wheat. Each step he took jarred her into his hard body.

Realizing she regained the ability to speak, she twisted and flailed. "Put me down! Put me down now!"

He squeezed her tighter, until she stopped yelling. "I don't think that will happen. I told you I'm taking you."

"Taking me where? You can't just take someone." Could he? She had a suspicion he may be one of the pirates she heard stories about and read in the papers. They did take what they wanted. "May I please put my clothing back on? Is Finn dead?"

Slowing inside a patch of thick-leaved vines, he whistled and a horse trotted up. Turning her, he lifted her up on the horse. She never rode without a saddle before. He jumped up behind her giving the horse a quick kick. It bolted off, and fear overcame her. Not just fear of falling to her death, but fear of what he intended to do with her. He jerked her back against his solid chest, holding her there with his left arm. Her fear of falling lessened, but others increased.

"Where are we going? My father is at the harbor," she said.

Loud, monstrous laughter exploded from him. "One more reason to stay clear of there then."

They rode fast, far from where she started. "Are you going to hurt me?" Tilting her head, she looked up at his face, but it revealed nothing. He stared ahead.

Following his eyes, he slowed the horse at some dunes. A massive ship sat anchored in the cove. Rowboats littered the beach. Men bustled about, loading items sitting on the beach to the boats, yelling at each other. He dismounted, dragging her with him. Directing the horse to the far left, a man, who looked local, roped it with the others he held.

"Aye, Spoon brought us quite a treasure," one of the dirty men hollered.

Many of the men ceased their activity, looking her way. Crossing her arms across her chest, she attempted to maintain some shred of modesty. They leered at her. She felt naked.

"This treasure isn't for you stinkin' scoundrels," her wild man stated. Pointing to the nearest boat, he commanded, "Get in."

Looking from the small vessel to the huge one out on the water, she panicked. Did he intend to take her there? Was he kidnapping her? Would she ever see her father again? Taking off in the direction they came, her neck snapped from the force of her hair being yanked from behind. Landing flat on her back in the sand, it took several seconds until she grasped that someone still held her hair. Her scalp ached.

Struggling to focus after the release of her tresses, she looked up the large body into the face of her captor. "Which part are you not understanding, Angel? I took you. You're mine. Get in the boat." The seriousness and anger reflected in his face halted any retort she considered giving. Sand hit her in the face as he walked away.

Rolling over, she pushed herself to her knees. She felt dizzy, pausing in that position. Only when she heard lewd comments from nearby men did her lack of attire, and the position she held, register in her aching, scrambled mind. Her shift caught under her knees, pulled below her breasts, leaving both of them swaying and on full display. Her dismay hadn't taken complete hold of her senses before two rough hands gripped under her arms. Slammed chest to chest with the wild one, she gazed into his mesmerizing eyes.

The narrowing of his eyelids, and the forming of a crease outside of each one, expressed his enjoyment of the situation well before she heard his boisterous laughter. "Maybe you, Li'l Angel, appreciate the attention of a bunch of drunken mates, but not while you're mine." Stomping to the boat, he dropped her inside. "Be aware of the state of your undress from here on."

"I requested you allow me to retrieve my dress... before you rode off with me," she countered.

Pinching her chin with his fingers, he captured and held her gaze. "You are not to disrespect me in front of the crew." He spoke quietly, for her ears only. "I'm not opposed to baring that creamy white ass for all to see. Pinkening it up would be highly satisfying."

Twisting free of his calloused, rough hold, she slid to the other side of the vessel. Stretching towards her, he gripped her arm, dragging her back to where he stood. "You don't listen very well." Hauling her to the side, he pushed her down, her stomach against it. Reaching down her legs, he yanked up her thin garment, baring her naked flesh for any to view. Appalled by his action, she tried to break free from him, bucking and twisting, but he pinned her head downwards with his man paw on the back of her neck.

The first crack of his palm against her bottom produced a howl from her that she didn't recognize as her own. Additional smacks rained down upon her poor backside. She shrieked, but he didn't relent. Only when he tugged her hair, directing her back on the bench did she realize it ended. Her vision blurred from tears, and she winced with each attempt she made to find a comfortable sitting position. Howls of laughter sounded in every direction. She had never been so humiliated.

"Let's go," he shouted. Men gathered at each boat, pushing them into the surf. Once cleared of the breakers, the wild one hoisted himself on the bench beside her. She watched as they left her only possible chance of escape, rowing closer and closer to the immense ship ahead.

Chants in song, lewd in nature, carried over the water from the neighboring vessels. The men maneuvering her boat remained silent. Sneaking a peek at her captor, she understood. He fixated ahead to their destination, his jaw firm, his posture threatening. It looked to her if any soul committed an act or sound not to his liking, it would be their last.

Crude climbing ropes hung over the side of the ship. The men making it there first vaulted from their boats onto these. They swung, kicked and fought with each other. In jest, she surmised, as they laughed and taunted each other. She toyed with the idea he didn't have any plan to take her aboard. She wore no shoes, and in her current state of undress, she couldn't climb.

Rowing beside the ship, he jerked her to her feet. Eyeing up the height, she stepped back, on top of his foot and into him. It looked so high from the water. It terrified her that he may expect her to climb the rudimentary contraption.

Shoving her forward, she fell to her knees, and he roared, "Go. It's time we sail."

She twisted her head wanting to admit her hesitancy to attempt such an endeavor, but his scowl frightened her more. Getting to her feet, she stepped to the side reaching for the rope. The little boat rocked away from her target, she missed the rope, falling into the sea.

Yanked up and out of the water, she came face to face with him. He dangled her in front of him like a doll. His warm breath hissed in her face. "You're wasting time." Slinging her on his back, he took hold of the rope, ascending the pair up the ship. "You may wish to hold tight if you don't want to find yourself back in the sea."

Tightening her arms around his neck, her legs around his middle, she closed her eyes, afraid to look either up, or down. His back muscles flexed against her chest each time he stretched and pulled them higher. Not expecting him to climb that distance so quickly, his booming voice startled her. "Let go now."

Opening her eyes, she found herself aboard the ship. Walking away from her, he yelled orders in every direction. The men did his bidding without question. Sprinting up a set of stairs, he joined another man overlooking the crew. They appeared engaged in a serious conversation. Unaffected by all the activity and noise, focused on whatever they spoke about, wild man had a definitive argumentative air about him. Both men were large in stature, and the whole scene sent her imagination into overdrive. These were two men who would make the most skilled officer cower.

The large sails inflated. The ship lurched, knocking her down and the ship sailed out of the cove. Song broke out among the men across the deck.

"What have we here?" Bony fingers gripped her elbow lifting her to her feet. The older man smiled his nasty teeth at her. "Look here, mates. Time for a li'l dancin'."

Men circled her, clapping their hands. They licked their sun split lips, staring at her wet undergarment, clinging to her body like a second skin. A palm slapped her backside. "Come on li'l lady, get to it," someone from behind demanded.

Other hands came at her, tugging on her, at her delicate frock. More clapping commenced, the crowd encircling her grew. "Dance… dance, dance," they screamed.

Crossing her hands over her chest, she stumbled in between them as they pinched, snatched, and shoved her. Before her terror engulfed her, she saw several men knocked to the floor. A huge fist made contact with jaws, faces. He stood beside her, sword drawn, the point angled under one chin near her. "Not this one, my friends. Not this one." Sheathing his sword, he instructed her, "Follow me, if you think you can without getting yourself in further strife."

Staying close on his heels, she followed him across the deck to a set of stairs leading below. The men continued to watch her, but no further remarks sounded. Opening a door, he waited for her to enter. A large desk filled the center, papers strewn atop. Stepping as far inside as she could, she turned to find him leering at her. His warm, gold eyes heated her in an unsettling way. She burned from the inside out, a feeling she never experienced before.

Marching in front of her, he put his hand in her hair behind her neck, tilting her face to his. His lips came down on hers fast, and hard. His breath became hers. Molding his lips to hers, his tongue pushed past her lips, caressing hers. The forceful, demanding kiss transformed into a gentle, sensual exchange. He licked behind her lips, over and around her teeth. She returned his attention, savoring the warmth and intimate exploration he initiated. An ache she didn't understand formed.

She shared a few kisses in her life, but nothing compared to this. His left arm encircled her waist, lifting her from her feet, without interrupting their mouth explorations. Carrying her across the room, he broke the kiss, staring at her with a heat in his eyes matching the fiery sensations she felt. Lowering them to a bunk, he held the stare, a shared understanding, an appeal for consent.

She knew this was wrong. She did. She just didn't care. The entire situation was wrong. The barbaric, alluring man took her, spanked her, forced her on a ship, and her only thoughts were of having his lips back on hers and easing the discomfort he created within her body. It scared her. It intrigued her. But she had no one to criticize or condemn her in that moment. She could do as she wanted.

Moving his head to her neck, he nuzzled it before he kissed it, progressing to deep, borderline painful lavishness. Though he sucked at her neck, she experienced a similar awareness in her core.

Sliding the drenched, ripped material off her shoulders, revealing her breasts, he immersed them in the same intense affection. He kissed, sucked, nipped, until she thrashed about yearning for more.

"Mm, what is your name, Angel?" he asked in the most masculine voice she ever heard. Even his voice affected her in a primal way.

"Pri… Priscilla," she panted.

Running his tongue under each breast, then circling each

nipple, she arched towards his mouth. "Priscilla. Was this Finn your husband? Such a lucky man."

She receded into the bunk, his words bringing her back to reality. "No. I am unmarried. Did you kill him? He was my escort."

His lips curled in a cunning smile. "No, Angel. I didn't kill him. Yet he may wish for it when he wakes up. He will have one hell of a pounding in his head." Stroking the side of her head, he ran his tongue along her jawline. "You are a virgin?"

Any attempt she made to remain unaffected by his lascivious tongue failed. He trailed it down her neck and along her shoulder interspersing kisses and nips. Closing her eyes, she disregarded any negative conceptions threatening to invade her mind and concentrated on the glorious madness his lips ignited throughout her entire body. If he thought her a virgin, would he stop? He couldn't. She needed him to soothe her suffering. A delightful misery she didn't understand. She heard pirates had no honor. But she wouldn't take a chance. She needed him to fulfill whatever he incited in her. "No."

His body shook with laughter. His rough, whiskered face rubbed against hers. "Do not lie to me, Angel."

How could the arrogant, lawless man be kind and caring with her? His concern for her virtue, the exact opposite of his menacing image, sent her desire soaring. She wanted the forbidden, the discovery, the adventure, she wanted the experience. "I do not lie," she hesitated, "Spoon?" He had a name. He had a past. Just as she.

Should she not have spoken his name? He withdrew. He eliminated all contact with her. Positioning himself on the other side of the small space exterminating any insane idea she imagined of being taken. In the truest sense, she wished to be taken. By him.

The smoldering lust he directed at her seconds prior vacated his eyes. All heat vanished and a chill engulfed her sending a shiver up her spine. "Did I grant you the right to call me by any name?" he cautioned. His face hardened, and his eyes bored into hers. "I think not."

"How would you like to be addresse–" she started. Flipping her onto her stomach, he ripped what remained of her undergarment.

Clamping her eyes shut, she gritted her teeth, awaiting the spanking she expected to receive. It didn't come. The bunk bounced indicating his departure. Listening, she heard his movement, but remained as she lay, eyes shut.

A slam of a trunk against the floorboard jolted her. "Get up. Your bottom displays plenty of attention as it is. So, I shall spare you this time," he stated.

Shifting upright, she sat at the edge of the bunk. A large trunk lay open in front of the desk. It contained many women's dresses.

Waving his hand over it, she looked from the chest to him, then back again. This angered him, as he hollered at her, "Get up, I said!" She stood, naked from the waist down. Gravity seized the remnants of material transporting it to her feet. He gritted out, "You are not to leave this cabin. But I won't leave you down here as you are—without me." Stretching out his right arm, he gripped her forearm, forcing her to her knees in front of the chest. "Damn it! Cover yourself, Angel."

He confused her. He seemed void of any tact. Gentle and kind, or impatient and brutish. And he spoke well, educated even. Which man did he wish to be? Running her hand along the gowns laid out on top, she realized they were expensive. Why did he have these? These were garments worn by wealthy women. What happened to the women?

"You're testing me, and my impatience grows. Any longer and I shall retract my decision to spare you additional discipline," he grumbled above her.

"I don't see any shifts. Stays? Stockings? Petticoats?" She lifted a few pieces, digging deeper inside.

Stomping his foot, he demanded her attention, which she gave. She held his amber eyes but averted hers at each validation he emphasized. "You *did not... don* those when I found you. And I d*oubt* you wore them sailing around the hot seas. Trust me, you *won't need or want* those where we are going and neither do the women we sell them to."

Dropping the garments, she stood. "Without a shift, or a petticoat, I will still be left quite exposed. My bosom shall be... uncovered. More than I wish." Years of hearing her mother's claims that a gentleman would never take her as a wife unless she behaved docile and practiced modesty echoed in her ears. She doubted her mother would approve of him regardless.

'Spoon' threw his head back and laughed like a mad man. She contemplated joining him in jest but reconsidered. Insolent and sarcastic behavior wouldn't persuade him to provide those. And more importantly, it wouldn't dissuade him from delivering 'additional discipline'. His laughter subsided. She discovered she liked how his eyes brightened and lifted when he smiled. "You, Angel, do have an ample bosom. I must agree."

She took a turn and stomped her feet. "Stop focusing on my breasts. Do you want me to get dressed or not? And what about all these clothes? You have been with all these women? Stolen them and brought them here as you have me?" Imagining him with other women infuriated her. Not one to usually get jealous, she recognized it. A ridiculous reaction under scandalous circumstances. But she assumed he completed the sexual liaisons he started with them. And he did not with her.

Seeing his eyes darken, and his jaw tighten, she stepped back. "You would do best to keep your thoughts in your head, not your mouth while here. I am attempting to treat you more as a guest, but you are trying me," he urged.

"A guest? Well, this guest wishes to depart this ship and return to her own!"

The amber in his eyes became burning embers, scorching her skin. Clamping his fingers around her neck, he led her to the door, then stalled. Grabbing the dress on top, he thrust it into her chest, without releasing her neck. "Put it on!"

Unable to bend down and step into the garment with his hand still around her throat, she stepped in with her right leg first, holding that side up. She repeated the same struggle with her left leg. His grip only tightened if she swayed. Whoever wore the dress matched her endowments in the chest area, but unlike her, they carried the same generous portions in the waist and hips and were much shorter in height. Lacing the front, she yanked it as tight as she could to close the opening, concealing her legs as best she could. Without a petticoat or stockings, they remained bare and fairly visible.

Directing her out of the cabin, he guided her down the corridor, down two small sets of steps, into a kitchen. The still, hot air made it hard to draw in a breath. Pots hung in every direction. "Bird. I'm putting a special guest back here for the time being. Not anyone, not a single soul is to enter," he yelled out.

She scanned the area, not finding another person, nor a 'bird'. Had he lost his mind? Could she push someone to that extreme? Her mother thought so.

"Yes, sir. I will not." An older man hobbled out from beside some stacked barrels.

Pressing her forward, her alluring abductor opened a small door in the corner. Forcing her inside, he took her to the back wall. A set of shackles hung halfway down. Forcing her to the floor, he caught her right wrist, lifting it up and into the contraption. "No. You can't be serious. You can't do this," she pleaded. His intentions clear, she panicked. Tears threatened to flow, but she refused. How dare he? Swinging her left arm, she slapped him before he caught it. "Stop it! This is wrong."

Both hands chained, he crouched in front of her rocking back on his heels. Almost as if he took great satisfaction in his restraint of her. Holding her chin, he held her to look at him, she closed her eyes. His lips crashed onto hers, moving them over hers. He smashed them into hers roughly. After the initial surprise of him mistaking her closing her eyes for an invitation to assault her lips faded, the same warm, uncomfortable feeling surfaced. The feeling made her want to succumb to his attentions, trusting somehow that he held the secret to alleviate her unfamiliar, but heavenly discomfort.

Resting her head against the wood, she allowed him access to her mouth. The more she submitted, the more she found she liked it. He reduced his aggression, licking and sucking her top, then her lower lip. Lifting her right leg, she bent it, rubbing against him. Feeling something hard, bulging from between his legs, she opened her eyes. It stretched the material and lay up against his lower abdomen. She realized what it must be. Shoving her leg back down, she turned her face away from him. She knew about the anatomy of men but hearing and experiencing were two different things. The reality of how close she came to engaging in sex with a stranger, a pirate, distressed her.

"What's wrong, Angel? Did you think you were the only one enjoying our interaction?" he asked.

Keeping her face turned, she didn't have a response. She stumbled way out of her comfort zone in his presence. Her mother and the women she kept company with detested their marital obligation, what if she did too? Here she thought she wanted this, believing so anyway, but what if she hated it?

"I'm thinking you may think twice before lying to me in the future. If I was nothing but a dishonorable man, I would take it from you, not caring if you received any enjoyment.

Priscilla." Hearing him address her by name, not Angel, she turned her head back, looking at him. "When you give me the gift of your virginity, I will take it not only with my pleasure a priority, but yours as well. As I plan on repeating it." Rising to his feet, he left her, left her to reflect on all that occurred since she left the protection of her father for a peaceful stroll on the beach that morning.

One would think he indulged in a day of rum and ale with his mates, but he couldn't blame either on his irrational decision. He got lucky Archer didn't call him out when he took notice of a woman on deck and the sails lifted. To make it worse, he had to go and rescue her from the crew under the watchful eye of their captain.

He needed to figure out how he planned to handle this without losing his dignity, and the respect of Archer and the men. He couldn't blame the crew for noticing her and wishing to enjoy the sight of her. Hell, that's what got him in this predicament to begin with.

Passing the beach, her hair caught his eye. The mass of radiant gold hung to her waist, and it sparkled in the sun. Dismounting, he snuck up in the thicket admiring her. The sea rushed her ankles and witnessing a woman of such beauty appreciating the sea, of something he loved as he did, fascinated him. Retaining it, her, dominated him. A woman never intrigued him as the sea did—until her.

Once she turned her head and he got a glimpse of the curiosity and enjoyment on her face, he wanted to be the source and reap the rewards of such gratification. He thought he appealed to her too. With her trapped in his arm at the beach, she looked into his eyes. She didn't shrink away from him in fear. And after their encounter in the cabin, then below, she proved it. Her reception to his physical attentions fueled his desire, but he feared he stole a lady, not a local of the island, and he planned to treat her as such. To a degree. When he ridded himself of her, he hoped she held some fond memories. He knew he would.

If he couldn't control her and her mouth, his intentions may fail. It was her choice.

Chapter 2

Fingers in her hair stirred her from a restless slumber. Her eyes flew open and she retreated pinning her back to the wall. The man from the kitchen stumbled backward landing on his bottom from a kneeling position in front of her, pulling some of her hair with him. "What are you doing?" she shrieked.

He trembled and stuttered. "I... am sorry, so sorry. Please don't tell, Spoon. Um, the quartermaster... Master Davies. Please."

Quartermaster? Master Davies. She figured he held a position of importance, but quartermaster? The poor old man looked more scared of her than she imagined ever being of him. "Well... answer me. What were you doing?"

Reaching behind him with shaking hands, he held out a tray with a cup of what she assumed was water, and a chunk of some form of bread. "I... I thought you may be thirsty. Hungry?"

Opening and closing her palm, she indicated she would take it, if she could. Her chains limited her range of motion, but she could touch her face so drinking shouldn't be an issue.

"Put the cup in my hand. Please." Setting the tray down, he did as she requested, and she drained it. "Are you going to tell me why you were touching me?"

Lowering his eyes, his head followed. He clasped his hands together, wringing them in his lap. "You are... are just so beautiful. Your hair is like, like, some of the sands I seen. I apologize, Miss. Honestly, I do."

"What is your name?"

"They call me Bird, ma'am." Peering at her, with his head still lowered, she noticed the cloudiness in his left eye. She wondered if he lost sight in it.

"Bird? That is your birth name?"

He chuckled. "Oh no, Miss." Unclasping his fingers, he pointed to his nose. "They call me bird because of this beak." He chuckled again. "They claim I descended from some ancient bird form because of my large nose."

Though she thought it rude of anyone to laugh at another's birth given physical traits, she couldn't help herself. His nose did remind her of a bird. She shared a laugh with Bird. He seemed harmless enough. She worried they didn't treat him right. An elderly and fragile man, tasked with cooking for the ship, in that sweltering kitchen. "So, Master Davies is the quartermaster of this ship?" she probed.

Glancing behind him, towards the door, he lowered his voice. "This ship, the Valiant, is captained by Archer. Davies has served as his quartermaster for many years and I hear he will be the captain of the Intrepid, Archer's other ship."

She considered this, thinking what to ask next. She had him talking, she wanted to obtain as much information as she could. It's not as if she expected Spoon or Davies to. "Is that where we are going? To his ship?"

Shrugging his shoulders, he rolled to his knees, positioning himself to stand. "They don't tell me when we stay, go. Or where we stay or go. I figure they go home when they got what they came for."

After minutes of Bird's bones cracking and his continual groaning, he made it to his feet. Bending for the tray and reaching for her cup, she stalled him. "Can I have a little more water? Please."

"I'm not s'posed to, but I will for ye." Taking the items, he limped out, mumbling more to himself than to her. "Always ration the water. Especially this early after leaving land. Always."

Returning with another full cup, she dreaded drinking it all. How did Davies expect her to relieve herself? "Bird. How long will I be shackled?"

Answering first with a shrug, he replied, "I don't know."

"How long does he usually leave women in here?" She hated that her voice conveyed her impatience, but she knew he had more to share.

"Finish your drink." He kept looking over his shoulder toward the doorway. After repeating his head turn several more times, he spoke so low she struggled to hear him. "They don't keep women in here. No women are aboard when we pull anchor. If they are…" He looked back again. "They just can't be."

He answered her questions, yet it only presented her with more. Deciding she couldn't stall him any longer, he was plagued with obvious fear, she worried he may fall over dead. Finishing her water she held the cup out as far as she could. "Thank you, Bird." Producing a polite smile, she whispered, "I'm Priscilla."

Returning her smile with what one could only describe as a toothless one, he took her cup. He dropped it more than once on his way out. Closing the door behind him, he left her with her continuous ponderings. Davies didn't take her for the entertainment of the crew. He couldn't use her as some form of negotiation for anything, as she didn't give her father's name or title. He didn't even know the name of the ship she arrived on. Trying to focus on the swaying of the ship and the creaks and bangs that went along with it, and not her increasing worries, she hoped Davies returned soon. To offer any form of explanation.

Without any further visits from Bird, the time dragged on. Her wrists ached, her arms as well from keeping them elevated at such a level. The sun lowered through the porthole, and she became restless thinking he may not return for her.

Hearing his voice out in the kitchen, relief rushed her first, then irritation. How dare he? The door burst open, followed by him ducking through the opening. "Did you have a peaceful afternoon, Angel?" His voice and his smile grated on her. Both smothered in sarcasm and arrogance. His masculinity, the rawness of him, enticed and thrilled her. And frustrated her more than anything he could say or do to her.

"Release me this instant!" She shook her chains. "Pleasant afternoon? You can't be serious! Let me loose."

He stood firm. His hair tied at the back of his neck, gold earrings hanging from his earlobes, his eyes became more prominent. She wished he didn't look at her as he did. Suffused in warmth from her scalp to her toes, concentrated in her middle, she shook her chains again.

Kneeling, out of reach of her, she kicked at him. He grinned. Unlike the other men aboard, he had straight, white teeth. "We need to have a little talk, Priscilla," he declared.

Hearing him speak her name again, her insides contracted. She shifted her body, wishing these sensations would leave her. There were too many other things taking precedence. "I agree. We do need to talk. Why did you take me? What do you plan to do with me? Are you going to chain me up every day?" she blurted.

The small space filled with his laughter. It aggravated her

that he laughed at her so much. "I meant I will do the talking. You agree and behave as I say."

Believing he didn't plan to harm her, her anger flourished. He may hold a position of authority on this ship, but she didn't answer to him. "I think not. I agreed that *we* need to talk. I won't agree to you doing all the talking… and me just obeying," she insisted.

"Tsk, tsk. My, my. Your father must have had to keep you over his knee as a child… or he needed to." Resting his elbows on his spread knees, he clasped his hands together. "If you wish to remain uncomfortable, so be it."

"Don't you talk about my father. Or my childhood. You don't know anything about me. What about you? Did you grow up without one? Is that why you have this false sense of authority?" As soon as the words passed her lips, she knew she made a mistake. But he had no right to mention her father. She had a wonderful father. He always bore the wrath of her mother to ensure she remained happy. Imagining how worried he must be, saddened her. He only gave in to her wishes that morning because she begged him. She hated knowing she caused him anguish.

A flicker of injury reflected in his expression before he rose. His voice took on a different tone. It held no emotion, just words. "I see you aren't ready to listen to reason. I can make the demands, Angel, I'm not the one shackled." He turned and left, pulling the door shut.

Damn her. He had no doubt she was a lady. Born into it. But it baffled him that she didn't cower or fear her current situation. She defied him in every encounter they shared. Verbally anyway. Her eyes, mouth and body sang a different tune. Knowing he could have what he wanted served as a blessing and a curse. He needed her to want him with the same fervor possessing him over her. The depth of passion that necessitated one going against their learned nature and submitting to their inherent nature. Her body responded and accepted it. Her mind and mouth—not yet.

Until she did, until he no longer feared her ability to hold her tongue and show him respect in and out of the presence of others, she stayed where he left her. He risked too much bringing her on board, but with the ship scheduled to depart, he didn't have a choice. He couldn't live with missing the opportunity of experiencing her. He wouldn't.

Every evening meal at sea, he shared with Archer. He hoped to have Priscilla by his side, but the probability of her impudence presenting itself quashed that notion. How did he expect her to act? He kidnapped her off a beach and forced her on a ship. Not to mention, he chained her to a wall. Did he believe he earned her loyalty and respect? Did he want it? Did he expect her to be amenable to him courting her? Which thinking about it, sounded like he wanted to. It could never be. He belonged to the sea. Did he suffer a wallop to the head, which escaped his memory, lessening his resolve?

He decided the sooner he sent her on her way, the better. When they stopped in Tortuga, he would do just that. Which gave him approximately five days to have her, enjoy her and be done with her.

Her stomach growled. Her throat hurt from dryness. Her arms went numb hours earlier. She assumed he planned to leave her there all night. That thought alone broke her. She no longer wanted to pretend to be brave. Imagining sleeping in the tiny, dark, rat-infested room frightened her. At night would they crawl on her? Would they bite her? Scratch her? Would she contract a disease and die aboard this ship, never seeing her father again?

The first few tears snuck out, rolling down her cheeks. Once she yielded to them, and her fear, she sobbed. She only had herself to blame. Not for the kidnapping and being on this ship, but for sneaking on her father's ship and convincing him to allow her to go to the beach. She wanted excitement and adventure in her life, just not the kind she found herself in.

Losing herself in her misery, she never heard the door open or Davies enter. His hands cupped each side of her head. The bands of the rings he wore were cool against her tear-soaked skin. The concern in his voice made her cry harder. "What is it, Angel? Are you hurt? Who hurt you?"

Continuing to weep, he released her hands, massaging her wrists. The ache in them grew as the blood returned. She bawled, attempting to pull them away from him. Putting one arm under her knees, he lifted her, wrapping his other arm around her shoulders, holding her head to his chest.

Carrying her out of the storeroom, she heard Bird's stuttering. "S-Sir. I d-di-did as you said. No soul entered th-tha-that room."

She felt Davies' growling voice in his chest, against her ear, before she heard him ask. And he asked in such a tone that demanded honesty, or death. "You are certain?"

"Y-Yes, sir."

Leaving the kitchen, Davies took the steps, walking down the hallway that led them back to the Captain's quarters. She continued to sniffle and gasp, but she no longer bawled like a baby. Sitting on the edge of the bunk, he stood and steadied her between his knees, untying her bodice.

Clawing at his hands, the soreness in her wrists hindered her ability to do much else, she sobbed again. "No. Don't, Davies. I'm not feeling romantic."

His fingers continued, unlacing the gown in expert time,

he slid it off her shoulders and down her body. He laughed. "Romantic." Lifting her off the ground, he placed her on the far side of the bunk, chuckling the entire time. "Romantic. That's a new one, Angel. I don't know if you will think it romantic once I am done with you." He took her wrists, caressing them.

"Why do you say such things? You don't mean them. You can't be wholly heartless."

Turning his back to her, he removed his boots. "Do you need to relieve yourself? I will step out and give you some privacy. I would bet my life Bird gave you something to eat and water. If you want more speak up before I get comfortable."

"I would like a moment to myself, please."

"I will give you two minutes, and then I'm coming back in. Don't get any ideas, I will be right outside the door."

She hurried off the bunk, took care of her pressing matter and scrambled back before he opened the door.

He came in, sat down and stripped off his shirt presenting her with a back covered in scars. Slashes. Someone mistreated him horrifically. She opened her mouth to ask, but he spoke first. "Don't mistake me for someone I am not. As you claimed earlier. I do not know you. You do not know me. Best if we keep it that way. We will enjoy each other." He stretched out beside her, keeping his back to her. "Rest. And you can call me Nathaniel."

Nathaniel. She liked it. It suited him.

Having never slept beside a man before, sleep eluded her. He fell asleep after he told her to rest. Listening to his steady breathing, she wished for him to roll over in her direction. She desired to study him without being under his watchful eye. Never had a man appealed to her like him. His looks appealed to her, no doubt. She wanted to know the man, his motivations, his aspirations. Who was he? In the past and the present.

As inevitable as sharing a sexual relationship seemed, she needed it to be more. And she would make it such. If it took her playing nice, she could do that. Not only would she attain what she needed, but it would keep her out of the chains.

He thought he could kidnap her, chain her, use her, deny her—that wouldn't work for her. She planned on enjoying him too, but she couldn't without understanding him.

Chapter 3

The men on this ship didn't start the day quietly. Loud movement and activity sounded in every direction. She jumped every time she heard the loud banging above her, worried they might fall through the ceiling and into her room. At some point, she fell asleep the previous night, and she must have slept soundly. Not seeing Nathaniel anywhere, she scooted off the bunk and slipped into her dress.

Looking out the porthole, the sun hadn't yet risen. Deciding to stay in Nathaniel's good graces, she didn't leave the room. Scanning the cabin, she located nothing to occupy her time. Maps and charts covered the desktop, but that didn't interest her.

The noise on deck continued. It made her uneasy, she had no idea what they were doing to cause such a disturbance. The door opened, and Nathaniel entered carrying a plate. His hair hung around his shoulders, his chest still bare and his eyes lit up when he spotted her. "You are awake. I thought you may be hungry. It's not much, but it's something." Setting the tray on the desk, she saw another chunk of some hard bread, and fruit. "I should have told you, but there's water in this pitcher on the shelf." He picked a cup up from the shelf and poured from a pitcher.

Another round of clamor clanged and bumped from above. "What is all that commotion?" she muttered.

"We completed our journey and are heading back. Maintenance and repair must be completed. If they want their shares, they need to complete their duties before we dock in Tortuga." Pulling a chair close to the desk, he motioned for her to sit in front of the plate.

"Tortuga? What do you want with me in Tortuga?" Her mouth went dry, she didn't think she could swallow anything, much less food. They sailed farther and farther away from her father. She didn't plan to return home with him, but what English presence would she find in Tortuga?

"Sit. Eat. We just stop over in Tortuga. My ship is in Port Royal."

He spoke so matter-of-factly. It irritated her. And she couldn't stop staring at his mouth. Recalling the way it felt, the way it tasted. "Well, my ship isn't in Tortuga... or Port Royal," she spat.

Gripping her shoulder, he pushed her into the chair. "Can I trust you to stay in here and behave yourself today? Or do I need to take you back behind the kitchen?"

Just the mention of chaining her back up in the kitchen made her tear up. Her wrists bore the bruises of yesterday's experience, and the knowledge that rats did inhabit the space terrified her. Twisting in her chair, away from him, she didn't want him to see her weak—again.

Stepping around the chair, he tried gaining her attention. "Priscilla. What is it? I know I have treated you badly. When we reach Tortuga, I will get you passage wherever you wish."

Shifting the other direction, she shook her head. Each time he spoke her name, it caused her body to react in ways she didn't understand. She couldn't imagine ever growing tired of hearing her name on his lips.

Kicking her chair out, he knelt between her legs. Grasping her shoulders, he pushed them back against the chair. Closing her eyes, she couldn't look at him. Tears flowed down her cheeks. He witnessed her vulnerability, and it made her sick. She didn't know who she was any longer.

"Tell me what upset you? I told you I would not return you to the chains if you behave. Has someone harmed you?" He spoke in a gentle, concerned voice. She liked it better when he conducted himself as a shameless man. Defying and resenting him came easier when he did. If he would keep his distance and not speak to her kindly, it could be less difficult enduring the barrage of emotions he incited within her.

"Just you." Opening her eyes, she looked into his gold eyes. Taking a deep breath, she hoped she appeared as controlled and dignified as she tried. "There are disease-carrying rats in there. I don't wish to contract one and die aboard this ship."

His body relaxed, followed by a seductive grin. "That is what had you so upset last night? The rats?"

"Why yes. Have you never heard of the plague?"

Shaking with laughter, he stood. "Yes, I have. There are many other concerns out here on the sea and in my duties. Much more pressing ones. Eat. Stay here."

"I am still a prisoner then? Confined to this room, just no shackles today?"

The harshness in his response made her tremble. "As long as I keep you… you are a prisoner. If you leave this room, I can do worse than chain you with the rats."

His lack of judgment and the whole spontaneity of taking her angered him. Not at her, but at himself. If she didn't look as she did, and didn't look at him as she did, his suffering might be alleviated. Everything in relation to her resulted in him acting out of character. He had no idea how he fell asleep last night knowing she lay behind him, nude. The battle in his conscience compared little to the battle that waged in his pants. Even at that moment. If he didn't vacate her presence as he did, he knew he wouldn't see any daylight that day. Maybe not the next either.

He needed to deny himself. A taste of her would never be enough. He knew his hunger for her was different and couldn't be sated. Her looks were deceiving. Angelic, innocent, and delicate, contrasted to the woman he brought aboard. The woman he left below deck gazed at him with lust in her eyes. She couldn't hold her tongue. He found it quite interesting that rats were the one thing that brought her to tears. And he hated seeing her big blue eyes fill with them. Keeping his distance became a necessity. He didn't want to ever imagine being the one who made her cry, but he knew he would.

She dreamed of romance and love. She associated sex with both, as any true lady should. He did not. He need not complicate her life more than he had.

The last two days she felt more like a prisoner than she did chained behind the kitchen. Nathaniel didn't bring her any of her meals after that first breakfast. He sent Bird. Nathaniel returned each night drunk. He stumbled, mumbled and smelled terrible. Once he managed to get all his limbs on the bunk, he passed out. Up most of the night due to his snoring, made worse from the rum, she managed to slip into a sound slumber in the early morning hours and awoke to find herself alone.

Bird attempted to make conversation when he brought her meals, but it pained her to witness how uncomfortable she made him. She didn't understand why Nathaniel avoided her. He took her. For what? To sit around below deck?

The third morning, she decided she wouldn't let it happen again. She obeyed his rule and stayed in the room, but she feared losing her sanity as a result of pure boredom.

Flipping on his back, his head fell in her direction. His eyes remained closed, his breathing steady. He truly had a magnificent look. The tanned skin, sun-lightened hair, straight nose, masculine chin and mouth, she loved admiring him. If anything, the last couple of days gave her time to evaluate. She yearned for adventure. One couldn't dream of more adventure. A rugged, striking man took her. He forced her on a pirate ship, and he, the pirate, wanted her. Or he did. But her adventure stalled. He ignored her. The one possible, most exciting journey she could find herself on, escaped her.

"Stop gawking at me like that," Nathaniel griped.

His voice and his words startled her. Her face heated. Unaware her eyes left his face, traveled down his solid chest and were currently focused on his stomach—maybe lower mortified her. Ever since her leg brushed up against his lower anatomy in the storeroom, her mind returned to that occurrence, often.

Bumping the wall behind her, she couldn't move any farther away from him. "I thought you were sleeping," she stammered.

"I was. I'm not now." Kicking his legs off the bunk, he once again put his back to her.

"Nathaniel. Can we talk? Please."

"I never gave you that name. I never gave you permission to address me with it," he grumbled.

"More the reason we should talk then. What would you have me call you?"

Pushing off the bed, he walked to the bookshelf, pouring a glass of water. "Nothing. I'm nothing to you, so don't address me."

Gritting her teeth, her temper flared. "Excuse me! What is your problem? You took me, put me in here, to what? Sit? That is shit!"

Slamming the cup on the shelf, water sloshed out over the sides. Rotating just his head, he scowled at her. His body rigid, his face hard, and she believed she saw his pulse beating in his temple. Dashing at her from across the room, she had no time to react. Situated in the bunk, her back against the wall, she had no escape.

Ripping the light cover from over her legs and out of her grip, he caught one of her kicking legs. Dragging her face down to the edge, he planted one of his heavy legs over her lower back, the other around her ankles dangling near the floor. Without warning, his palm collided with her bare butt. He continued, all landing on the same cheek, the same spot. They came at a steady beat. She first tried to count them, not wanting to cry, but they seemed to come harder and quicker.

Pinned the way he had her, it constricted any possible movement. Her torso lay flattened into the mat from the weight of his large thigh, making it difficult to even turn her head. As much as she didn't want him to know his little act of aggression hurt, it did. He seemed determined to target just one spot, as if waiting on her to beg him to stop. The over-whelming need to scream and cry out worsened with each strike, but she wouldn't give him the satisfaction. She wouldn't be his obedient little doll, or whore, or victim.

Tears escaped. Not only from the pain she endured, but from her fortitude, and the concentration she forced into holding her eyes shut so tight. He slowed, and she heard him breathing heavy. Maybe his hand felt some of what her left cheek did. She hoped he did wear himself out.

Resting his hand on her bottom, she feared he may lift it and commence the punishment. He didn't. Several minutes passed, and he didn't move. He didn't make a sound. Taking his legs off her back and from around her ankles, he slid off the bunk onto the floor. She made no attempt to lift her head, or move her body, but she felt him brush against her left leg.

Placing his hands on her waist, he lifted her off the bed, turning her to face him. His golden eyes took on a glow of fiery embers. Cupping her face, he wiped her wet cheeks, resting his hands on them before he moved and placed her on the bed. Guiding her legs apart, he positioned himself between them, pulling her to the edge. Lowering his face to her most intimate parts, she yelled, "No! What are you doing? That's vile. Stop." She slapped his head with both her hands, until he gripped them, holding them to her sides.

"Be quiet. Trust me, you won't think it's vile in a few minutes." His breath touched her, the warmth of it generating a rush of heat throughout her entire body.

Squirming, she begged him. "Don't. You can't. This is wrong." She knew her voice denoted no honest request. What-ever he intended to do, she wanted it. Her body became so taut she thought she might break if he quit, and break if he didn't.

Burying his nose at the top, he dipped his warm, wet tongue into her very center. Her legs clamped around his head. It may be wrong, but her body felt more alive than she ever thought possible. Not only did it come alive, it reacted as if it became a separate entity. Swiping his tongue up through her folds, her insides contracted, and she wanted and needed something, but what?

"You want more, Angel?" he asked in a husky voice, inducing additional spasms to her thighs and core. She ached for him to continue, to take her where her body so willingly wanted to go. "Don't worry, you don't have to speak it. Your body is telling me." He put his mouth on her again, licking. He licked her low, to the top, concentrating there. He lapped at her, slow and gentle. A pressure built inside her. She moaned, turning her head from side to side. He flicked his tongue, fast, and she didn't know if her body betrayed her.

She trembled as ecstasy coursed from her center to each limb and back again. She lingered in a state of bliss, yet she felt there was more. The ensuing shudders encompassed swells of pleasure accompanied by almost painful jolts. She didn't want it to end. She hurt for more.

Clawing his hair, she hadn't realized he released her hands. She gripped his hair, pulling him closer, wanting him to relieve her agony. His lips closed around the top again. He sucked her. Not hard, but just enough that her body went lax before it spasmed with surges of pleasure erupting and rendering her defenseless to her body's reactions. Her mouth fell open. She became lost in sensations, powerless to prevent them. Each time her body relaxed the smallest amount, he sucked her again and it started all over.

She gasped for breath, he moved his face away from her, remaining in the same position. "Angel, I want you to remember how you feel right now." Lying limp on the bed, her body fatigued, she glanced at him. His expression appeared serious, but his hands were at his waistband pushing his pants down. He grinned at her. "Look away. I don't want you seeing it before you have had a chance to enjoy it. You can. You will. Most likely not today… your first time. I'll make it quick."

Nothing could make her deny him at that moment. Nothing. She wanted him to feel as good as he made her feel. Could she? He rubbed her right hip, up her side to her arm. He rubbed it before he gripped it. Before she had a chance to comprehend what he said, he entered her. Lurching away

from him, from it, she couldn't breathe, nor speak. It hurt. It felt abnormal.

Squeezing her arm, he spoke gently, "Look at me." Inside her, he stilled, allowing her body time to adjust and accommodate him. "Angel, look at me." The pain subsided, but him, it didn't belong there. It needed to get out of her. "Priscilla. I said look at me."

She did as he directed. He loosened his grip on her arm, but didn't release it. Beads of sweat covered his chest, and strands of hair stuck to his forehead and around his cheek. His eyes were soft, yet intense, she saw his struggle in them. The restraint he put himself under, if anything close to the sweet torture she felt minutes earlier when her body begged for more, astounded her. His patience and concern stunned her.

"Keep your eyes on me," he instructed. "I've breached you now. The worst is over. It will only get better from here."

Focusing on the intimacy the two shared at that moment caused emotions to surface she didn't expect. She felt as if she would do anything for him. Never had she cared enough for another man, besides her father. She belonged to Nathaniel now, and she wanted to. Her body knew before her mind did. She wanted to share this with him again, and again.

Moving away from her, he withdrew some from inside her. Though it continued to feel odd, the sensation changed. No longer painful, but somewhat pleasant, as he slid slowly different areas were stimulated. Gazing at him, the act itself went along with her knowledge and appearance of him, but his movements and execution didn't. He may not look like the gentlemen she was accustomed to, but the tenderness and consideration he showed her she doubted she would share with another man.

Looking at him, the determined set of his jaw, the glow in his eyes, and the tension in his tanned physique had her craving the ecstasy he gave her minutes before. He continued to withdraw a little, then glide back in. "Are you good?" he asked.

"I am." Her voice breathy, her body tensing, her body climbed to the blissful peak she now knew he could take her. Continuing his steady, slow thrusting, he rubbed her where he sucked her earlier, and she reached a state of rapture again. He moaned, pumping her quicker. Groaning loudly, he laid on her. His head on her right shoulder, his breath in her neck.

Both panting, neither spoke for several minutes. "Are you hurt, Angel?" he asked.

Wrapping her arms around him, she answered, "No. Far from it." She wondered if it would be like this every time. She couldn't imagine it being any better.

Lifting himself out of her arms and off of her, he pulled his pants up and stood. Picking his shirt up from the floor, he put it on, not looking at her. "I will have Bird bring you some water to wash up." He went toward the door.

He intended to leave her? Again? Did she do something wrong? Sitting up, she asked, "Where are you going?"

"I have a crew to command." His voice sounded hollow, like his words. His dismissal of her and the experience they shared pained her.

"I do not wish to be alone in here all day again. Can you please take me up on deck?"

Without responding, he walked out of the room, slamming the door behind him. She wished she could remain unaffected, but she couldn't. Curling up on the bed, she cried. She wished he wouldn't have treated her with such kindness if his true intent was to use her and treat her poorly. She needed to remember who he was. A pirate. A thieving, selfish, ruthless criminal.

What a mistake. Where did his resolve go? His decision to keep his distance until they reached Tortuga and he could unload her failed. Her response to him conjured unfamiliar feelings in him. Her pleasure, her pain, her safety became priorities. He didn't like it. He didn't need it.

Chapter 4

Priscilla didn't fulfill her goal of sharing meals and conversations with Nathaniel. He continued to drink in excess each evening, return to the cabin, and pass out. They did repeat the passion they shared each morning before he hurried out.

She no longer knew if it was a blessing or a curse. Sitting alone all day and much of the evenings, she had nothing to occupy her mind except reminiscing about him and their love-making. She wished he would allow her time to learn about him, not just his body. Each time they enjoyed and explored each other surpassed the previous one. He became all she thought about... all she dreamed about. Her body, mind and heart craved the minute amount of time he gave her and the attention he bestowed on her when he did.

Writing one morning at the desk, anything to occupy her time, amplified shouting, and increased activity came from above. Had they arrived? Arrived in Tortuga? Leaving the desk, she hurried to the porthole, but didn't see anything, but blue ocean. The door burst open, and Nathaniel rushed in.

Sitting on the bunk, he grabbed his boots, pulling them on. "Stay here, Priscilla," he commanded.

"Why? Do I not get to leave the ship?" she whined.

Marching across the room, he retrieved a jacket, slipping it on. "Did you not hear what I said?"

Her irritation grew. Why did he keep her around if he only planned to avoid her, and ignore her after each time they were intimate? "I heard what you said! I didn't like it! Why don't you just release me here? It's apparent you don't want me."

He snarled at her, "I don't have time for this! Do as I say."

Running over to him, she fisted her hands and punched his back. "I'm tired of this! Release me, please. You got what you wanted from me, let me go now. You can't even look at me."

Twisting around, he gripped her wrists, pushing them to her sides. Leaning down, his face inches away from hers, he said, "Stop it. You are behaving like a child. I'm doing what I can to keep you safe."

"I haven't been safe since the day you took me off that beach," she muttered.

His anger burned in his eyes. The intensity frightened her. She attempted to back away from him. He released one of her wrists, but held the other and dragged her out of the room. She held hope her pleas persuaded him to let her leave the ship, but he headed to the galley. The fear of returning to the storeroom with the rats terrified her. "No! Please don't. I will do as you said."

Ignoring her, he pulled her along. Reaching the kitchen, he took her to the small room, pushing her towards the wall holding the chains. "Get over there. Don't make this more difficult than it has to be."

Her jaw tensed. She knew the tears were coming. "Please, Nathaniel. I promise I will adhere to your wishes."

Pointing to the floor by the shackles, he wouldn't meet her stare. "Do it!" he yelled.

Tears trickled from her eyes. This Nathaniel she couldn't reach. Stepping over to the wall, she plopped to the ground, holding her wrists out in front of her. Continuing to avert his eyes, he took each wrist placing it in a metal restraint. Her tears flowed, but she wouldn't give him the satisfaction of reducing her to a sniveling child. "I hate you!" she screamed when he reached the door.

Without looking back, he stated, "No, you don't."

She might. She wanted to.

Hearing and feeling the ship anchor, her disappointment mounted. She didn't want to leave Nathaniel, but she tired of not seeing the light of day, and never leaving the small quarters. She knew nothing of Tortuga, so she couldn't understand his reluctance to hold her on the ship.

She relied on him now. Did he confine her because he worried she may attempt to escape? She didn't believe that. He showed little affection for her. Except in bed. If that was so, why didn't he relieve himself of her now when he had the opportunity?

Bird didn't come to see her this time. A silence descended upon the ship. How long would she be in this room? She yelled out to Bird several times over the course of the day, but she heard nothing. As the sun lowered, her stomach rumbled, and her throat ached from being without any water. After sitting in silence all day, it stunned her when shouts and movement erupted all around her at once.

She heard men crawling up the side of the ship. Orders were shouted in every direction. Gunfire came next. She didn't know what occurred. She didn't know if anyone besides

Nathaniel knew about her or her location. Pulling on her chains, she knew she couldn't escape. She tested them many times. Her wrists were raw and bruised, but she continued to try as voices and footsteps came closer.

The door flew open. A thin, dirty man gaped at her. He opened his mouth to speak revealing a mouth containing only broken teeth. "Well, well, what do we have here?"

Tugging at her restraints, she fought to free herself. Sliding back against the wall as far as she could, she screamed, "Get out of here! Leave me be!"

An eerie, haunting cackle gurgled out of his throat. "Hackett didn't mention there might be human treasure on the Valiant." Dropping his weapon, he strode closer reaching towards her left leg. She kicked at him with her right, catching him in his ribs. "You li'l bitch." He raised his hand, slapping her across the cheek. Her head snapped with the force. "Where's the key? If you think chains are bad, you just wait."

Scrambling around the small space, he searched for a key, she supposed. Even if she knew its location, she wouldn't tell. This ship must be the target of a raid. She had never heard the name 'Hackett'. What would become of her now? The activity she heard previously onboard ceased. How many of the crew went ashore?

He tossed items about. Many struck her. She curled up and away from him as far as she could. Gripping her hair, he yanked her head towards him. Spit flew from his grotesque mouth as he spoke. "Where's the key?"

It happened so fast. She thought she noticed movement behind him, but he held her head firm, forcing her to look at him. His eyes bulged and a silver blade burst through his mouth. Blood spurted, drenching her. Closing her eyes, she screamed. His hand still caught in her hair left her unable to shield her face.

Somehow, her hair got freed. She kept her eyes closed,

moving her head from side to side, screaming. Hands cupped each side of her face. She yelled louder.

"Stop. Stop, Priscilla. You are safe now," assured Nathaniel's familiar voice. Running his hands over her hair, he addressed her in a calm and soothing tone, "Keep your eyes closed. I'll release you and get you out of here."

She whimpered when she lost his touch against her head, but he unchained her, massaging her wrists and hands. Gripping her left elbow, he assisted her to her feet. Her toes touched a body, but she kept her eyes shut. He guided her out of the room, and she heard the door shut. "You can open them now, but don't be alarmed. We will get you cleaned up. Just look straight ahead."

It scared her. What she would see, but what she felt all over her body horrified her the most. She knew she wore another human's blood. Leading her up on deck, she assumed they extinguished all threats. Nathaniel spouted off to a couple of men who ran to do his bidding. They brought buckets of water, placing them near him. "Close your eyes again. I'm going to pour these on you," said Nathaniel.

Doing as he directed, the tenderness with which he rinsed out her hair, and the attention he provided to her ears, her neck, her fingers, and feet comforted her. She didn't know how many buckets he poured on her. She didn't care. She trusted when he finished, she could try to forget the incident altogether, knowing he washed all evidence from sight.

Holding her hand, he took her to the steps that led back to their quarters. He stopped there. "Slide your dress off your shoulders. I will let you put on my coat. We will leave your garment," Nathaniel advised.

Scanning the ship, men were in every direction, but the wet dress was heavy and uncomfortable. Her hand shook as she lifted it toward her shoulder. Nathaniel removed his coat. Watching her trembling hand, he took it in his. Holding it for a moment, he released it and slid her dress from each shoulder. He assisted in freeing her arms from the gown. Placing his coat on her, he knelt, pushed her dress to her feet and directed her to lean on his shoulders while he ridded her legs and feet of the saturated material.

Standing in front of her, he kissed her forehead. His lips lingered there, and she took a deep breath. She experienced tenderness with him, but only when he lay with her. As much as she wanted to be angry at him, he comforted her, and she realized she craved it. From him.

Wrapping his arm around her, he held her tight against him, shielding her from any ogling from the crew. He steered her down the steps to the sanctuary of their room.

Feeling her soft body against his side did little to douse the rage smoldering throughout him. Never had he felt relief the way he did when he found her, alive. Killing that one man did little to extinguish his fury. The entire day, the entire plan of action, made no sense. He knew something wasn't right from the activity of the crew and the orders given by Archer. Once he ensured Priscilla's safety and comfort, he intended to speak to Archer.

Opening the door, he found Archer sitting behind his desk, his legs crossed atop it. Priscilla turned into his chest, whimpering.

"You are safe. Come on, let's get you to the bunk," Nathaniel said leading her to the bed. He hated to release her, but he had to. Archer made no attempt to stand and greet them. If possible, he leaned his chair back farther. A thick air of haughtiness enveloping him.

Priscilla clawed at Nathaniel as he pushed her to the bunk. Bending forward, Nathaniel whispered, "Nothing will harm you. Again. Scoot back against the wall. Let me talk to the captain."

The fear in her eyes disturbed him. He wanted nothing more than to remove it. Forever. Cupping the side of her head, his nose in her hair, he breathed her in before turning and facing Archer. "You have not convened here in the 'Great Cabin' since we left Nassau, Captain," Nathaniel prodded.

Rubbing his beard, Archer made no other motion. Nathaniel walked across the room, standing in front of the desk. The captain didn't look at him as he spoke, devoid of his mindset or intention. "I do believe this space has been occupied since then. Has it not?"

Though he and Archer maintained a profitable relationship over the years, each man holding the other in high regard, Nathaniel knew when he took Priscilla that he created a plethora of complications he would be accountable for. It shocked him that Archer had not broached it with him before then. "This is your ship, Archer. This cabin belongs to you," stated Nathaniel.

Lifting his feet from the desk, Archer slammed them on the floor and stood. Banging his palms on the desk, he leaned over it, narrowing his eyes at Nathaniel. "Yes, it is. I am the captain. And all that sail under me and with me honor this." Twisting his head, he gazed in Priscilla's direction. Taking a few steps towards her, Nathaniel moved in front of him, placing himself between Archer and Priscilla. "Every man, including you, understands and signs our Articles."

Regret seized Nathaniel. He took advantage of his friendship with Archer. "Yes. Even I, Captain."

Archer waved his arm in Priscilla's direction, Nathaniel gripped it.

Jerking free, Archer snickered. "The two times I have caught a glimpse of the lady that you place such value in that you dishonored me and the crew, she looks like a drowning rat."

"Don't," warned Nathaniel.

"Miss. Miss, please look at me when I address you." Archer directed his words to Priscilla, but he didn't move any closer to her.

Nathaniel intervened, "After being attacked earlier, I doubt she will answer."

"Don't interrupt me! My patience has waned." Stepping to his right, Archer attempted to gain her attention. Nathaniel stepped to his left blocking his action. Archer announced, "You will not sail with the Valiant to Port Royal. You are dismissed of all service under me."

"My shares from this loot should pay the remainder of the Intrepid. She is my ship now," countered Nathaniel.

"Agreed. But you won't be receiving any share. Get your woman and get off my ship." Archer clutched Nathaniel's left forearm. "If you wouldn't have raced back to save her, this may have been all avoided. You left me no choice."

Hearing Archer's declaration confirmed his suspicions. Pulling his knife, Nathaniel grabbed the back of the captain's head in one hand, holding the knife under his chin with the other. "You knew Hackett was in Tortuga!" he yelled. "You orchestrated the whole raid today in the hopes they would kill her or take her?" His voice spoke the depth of this betrayal. Dropping both arms, he strode to Priscilla, taking her hand. Keeping himself between her and Archer, he took her to the trunk. "Choose a dress and put it on."

"You know there are to be no women or boys onboard, Davies. Or perhaps I should address you as 'Spoon'. I welcomed you into this crew. You were nothing more than a powder monkey. I gave you more opportunity than you ever would have had with Hackett." Brushing his hands over the arms of his coat, Archer continued, "Though I haven't confirmed with the lady if you brought her aboard without consent, as you know that punishment is death, I don't need to. It is obvious where your heart lies now. Why a man in love wants to keep a ship he will never sail, I do not understand, but the Intrepid waits for you in Cooper's Cove at Port Royal."

She trembled to such an extreme he had to help her dress. He wished Archer wouldn't have mentioned 'love'. He planned to procure the Intrepid and continue pirating. Settling down with a woman didn't coincide with this. Archer had been lenient with him, and for that he was thankful. Their Articles stipulated any woman aboard, even if she engaged in consensual sex, goes overboard.

Chapter 5

Priscilla's entire body ached. Her left cheekbone hurt the most, followed by her wrists, but everything hurt. It could most likely be attributed to all the shivering and the excessive tension. Her head throbbed. She couldn't focus on much for any extended amount of time. Her confusion over Nathaniel and his actions compounded after hearing the exchange between him and Archer.

Did he love her?

One minute he behaved as if he hated her. The next, he protected her. Now she learned he broke their 'Articles' by taking her in the first place. A crime punishable by death. Not that she would ever admit he took her against her will. She didn't want him dead. She just wanted him. Or she did. Maybe.

Departing the ship, several members of the crew joined them, leaving their service under Archer. A few of the men tried to engage Nathaniel in conversation regarding his plans for reaching the Intrepid and any possible departure schedule, but he silenced them. His abrupt reply advised them they would meet mid-day tomorrow.

Walking under a full moon, a light breeze blew sending additional chills down her spine. Nathaniel draped his coat over her shoulders. Prior to leaving the pier, her impression of Tortuga was that it wasn't a place she imagined herself in. Music, laughter and lewd comments filled her ears. Turning right down a narrow street they encountered a crowd of drunken men. Nearly nude prostitutes hung themselves in rude positions over balconies and doorways. Every couple of steps Nathaniel shielded her from stumbling and wild punches by brawling men. She had no clue where he intended to take her, but she prayed far away from that ruckus.

"*Mon amie*, Davies!" yelled a dark-haired woman as she darted from a doorway embracing him. "*Dois-je demander Madame Sabine?*" she asked in a thick French accent.

He kept pace, barely acknowledging the woman. "No, Lisette. Later."

Just the thought of him being with women like her, bothered Priscilla more than she cared to ponder. She lacked the experience these women did. Did he prefer that type of partner?

He gave her a pair of shoes before they departed the ship, but they were several sizes too big. Sand, and whatever else she walked through, found its way in and it irritated her skin with each step. She planned to keep any complaints to herself and focused on getting distance between Nathaniel and the whores.

Making their way out of the town, the men who left the ship with them stayed back. She and Nathaniel walked along dirt paths across flat land in silence. She wanted to just lie down. And sleep. Not think about what transpired or anything else.

Her body protested with each step she took until she finally darted away from him and gave in. Retching caused more pain. Every part of her ached.

Rubbing her back, he sympathized, "Come along. It's not much farther. I am sorry to make you walk so far after all that occurred today."

Dry heaving a few more times, she straightened. "Where are we going?" she asked.

"Somewhere safe. Somewhere you can stay while I go and retrieve my ship."

He planned to leave her? "No. I want to go with you," she asserted.

Without responding, he urged her to continue down the path. He led them off the path, across a field, and into some trees on higher ground. Not paying much attention, she followed. It took all she had to place one foot in front of the other.

She thought of nothing on the long trek, only of reaching a destination. Her thighs burned with each step as they traveled higher. Coming upon a fenced section, he took them to a gate and opened it. Waiting on her to pass through, a male voice called out from darkness ahead. "You're back early. Ma wasn't expecting you for at least another week."

A young man approached them and lowered his firearm. Nathaniel put his arm around Priscilla's waist, pulling her against him. "I will be leaving again tomorrow."

"Not without me, right? You said when I reached seventeen years. I am almost eighteen," the young man said as he walked alongside them.

Nathaniel's reply came quick and harsh. "Not right now, Henry. I have other things to tend to."

The young man halted and stomped his foot. He huffed, remaining in the dark.

Hearing chickens, Priscilla saw a chicken pen. Glancing around, she noticed several small structures and other penned areas. Illumination in the distance turned out to be a home. It had a large covered front porch. Guiding her up the few steps, Nathaniel opened the door leading her into a fair-sized room containing a table and chairs, a large fireplace, and a cooking preparation area against the back wall.

A small woman darted out a door from the right. Dressed in her bedclothes, she looked panicked until she set her eyes upon Nathaniel. "You are here," she exclaimed as she studied Priscilla. "What have you done?" She questioned him, but her eyes never left Priscilla.

He looked at the woman following her eyes to Priscilla's swollen face. "No, I did not do that. One of Hackett's." Filling a cup with water, he placed it on the table, tossing some bread there as well. "Sit down, Priscilla. Drink. Eat." Tension emanated from him on a level she hadn't felt before. He didn't make eye contact with her, or the other woman. *Who was this woman? Was this his family?*

Grabbing his upper arm, the woman shook him, imploring him to look at her. "Hackett is here? On Tortuga?" she demanded.

Squeezing her shoulder with his right hand, they looked into each other's eyes, a shared understanding and pain passed between them. "I do not believe so. I think he and his men came over from Hispaniola long enough to execute Archer's plot and take whatever prize he left them for doing so," assured Nathaniel.

A multitude of emotions displayed in her eyes, but her voice indicated nothing but disbelief. "What? Why? Archer and Hackett... formulated an incursion on the Valiant?" Backing away from Nathaniel, the woman bumped into Priscilla. She pinned her with her eyes. "Because of her? She is Hackett's?" Her tone and pinched face revealed her disdain for Priscilla and her presence.

Priscilla darted for the open door. Nathaniel clutched her

wrist, holding her back. "You aren't going anywhere," he announced. "And no, Lydia, she was not, is not Hackett's."

Glancing over her shoulder, Priscilla watched Nathaniel look from her to the other woman. And back again. Lydia, as he addressed her, turned her head away when she caught Priscilla's eyes. Priscilla did the same. "Why are we here? Why did you bring me here?" yelled Priscilla.

Jerking her to the table, he clamped his fingers over her shoulders, pushing her into a chair. "You will do as I say. My options are limited. Eat," he barked.

Bounding to her feet, she faced him. "Your options? What about mine?" Where she mustered the bout of energy, she had no clue. "I will not stay here with your… wife. I'd rather stay in town with your whores."

A mighty tic in his jaw pulsed. She assumed with his heart-beat. His eyes narrowed and he clutched her wrist hard. Twisting her around, her face to the table, he pushed her arm up her back forcing her forward. Throwing up her skirt, he slapped her exposed bottom until she sobbed. Tugging her upright, he towed her to a door to the left. Opening it, he shoved her inside. "Do not give me anymore trouble tonight. Get some sleep," he growled before slamming the door.

She stood where he left her and cried in the dark room. Fatigued, hungry, shamed, angry, confused, hurt, she couldn't think straight. Nathaniel and Lydia argued on the other side of the door, but she couldn't concentrate enough to hear what they said. Jealousy raged through her enflaming her fury. She didn't want to care about him, but she did. The thought of him being with another woman, married to another woman, devastated her. What a stupid realization that was. The hit to her face earlier must have messed with her mind.

"Why are you crying? You can share my bed," spoke a young female voice from deeper in the darkness. "I am Alice."

Startled at first, as she didn't consider she may not be alone, she stopped crying. Her eyes adjusted to the dimness. She could make out a bed, and a figure sitting in it, but not much else.

"What is your name? I'm twelve. Did you meet my brother Henry? He is seventeen," continued Alice. "Why don't you at least sit? They will probably quarrel for quite some time."

Moving to the bed, she sat on the edge. "I'm Priscilla. Do your parents argue often?"

Pushing a pillow towards Priscilla, Alice replied, "No. My parents never argued."

Kicking the much too large shoes off her feet, she stretched out on the bed by Alice. Nathaniel and Lydia moved from the front room onto the porch. She heard raised voices, but not what they said. Priscilla didn't ask him to bring her there. She didn't ask for any of this. She closed her eyes, relaxing and rejoicing over how good it felt to be off her feet.

A hand patted her shoulder. "Ma says you need to get up now. Things need to get done."

Opening her eyes, Priscilla saw a young girl dressed in a simple dress. She wore her bright orange hair in braids. Her giant blue eyes displayed her angst. Sunlight shone in through the window behind the bed.

Priscilla couldn't remember anything after she lay down the previous night. "Alice?" she asked the girl for confirmation. She didn't get a good look at the girl the night before.

"Yes, Priscilla. I'm Alice. If Ma comes back inside and you aren't up…" Lifting herself to her toes, she peered out the window. "Come on. I poured you some water. It is on the table. And I stuck some bread in your apron pocket."

SHERI LYNN

Priscilla's usual morning routine didn't include rushing around to do anything. Once on her feet, she went to the water pitcher on a chest with the intent to wash up. Lifting the pitcher to fill the bowl, she glimpsed Lydia rushing into the main room carrying two pails.

Lydia's demeanor hadn't improved overnight. She barked at Priscilla, "No time for that. You'll have to get up earlier. Come here."

Even Priscilla's own mother didn't talk to her in such a manner. Approaching Lydia, she scanned the area beyond the open door. Several darker skinned individuals moved about carrying buckets and tools.

"Where is Nathaniel?" she inquired.

Thrusting a basket at her, Lydia instructed, "Go fetch the eggs."

Eyeing the basket, Priscilla asked again, "Where is Nathaniel?"

Continuing with her tasks, Lydia emptied portions of the pails to different containers. She didn't appear to have any interest in interacting with Priscilla, nor responding to her question. Alice tiptoed out of her room and out the front door.

Minutes passed. Once Lydia emptied one bucket, she reached for the other. Noticing Priscilla, she snapped, "Why are you still standing there. Go get the eggs as I asked."

"You didn't ask. You ordered," responded Priscilla. Glancing back out the door, she stated, "You have all this help here, why do you expect me to do a task they should complete?"

Lydia's back stiffened. Spinning around facing Priscilla, she seethed, "You will not disrespect or address our neighbors in such a way. We all work together for the good and survival of us all." Banging her palms on the table, she leaned forward, glaring at Priscilla. "The ones that come on a regular

52

basis, earn a wage. There are no slaves on or near my property."

"I apologize for my assumption. The rumors circulate that the colonies obtain and use many from the islands. I just expected you practiced the same here." Priscilla sincerely regretted her comment. She grew up with a caretaker and servants, but on many occasions, they were more family to her than her birth family. "I know better than to put any trust in the stories and gossip among any acquaintances of my mother. I spoke without thinking."

A softness came into Lydia's eyes. Lifting her hands from the table, she stood and wiped her hands on her apron. "There is truth in the slave trade. It is deplorable, and an immoral means for any Christian to profit from." She slid a chair out from the table. "Sit for a moment and drink. You must be thirsty. I'll get some bread. Some fruit."

Making her way around the table, Priscilla took the offered seat. She watched as Lydia gathered the food and noticed how pretty she was. Her brown hair pulled into a knot at the nape of her neck made the slenderness of her frame all more visible. To be such a diminutive woman, she carried herself with much strength and attitude.

Setting the tray down, she asked Priscilla, "Where is your home? Your family?"

Tentative to answer any questions, she didn't trust anyone. Especially with the truth. How could she? She knew nothing about Nathaniel. The man she should most likely fear and despise, yet she didn't. Did Nathaniel leave her here? With his wife? "I lived in Charles Town. I found life as my mother laid out for me... to be boring."

This admission had Lydia laughing. A sweet, joyous sound regardless of its obvious sarcasm. "I figured there must be more to you than just beauty. Nathaniel craves a life filled with excitement and adventure as well. He tends to act before thinking and the results can be quite damaging to not only himself, but to those who love him."

That this woman complimented her, heartened her. But Priscilla comprehended the negativity behind her last statement directed at her. Both women currently existed under unusual circumstances, with a high probability of volatile consequences. "Where is Nathaniel?"

"He and Henry left at first light to go get the Intrepid. Did he not tell you this?" Lydia asked in an empathetic voice as she took a seat across the table.

The bread Priscilla stuck in her mouth seemed to swell as she grasped the fact that he left her there. He didn't share a bed with her either. Did he share Lydia's bed? Picking up the cup, she guzzled the contents, but the bread just moved further down her throat. Lodging itself there.

Lydia took her hand in hers. "He left you here to ensure your safety. As he has always done for me. No woman's face should ever bear bruises as yours does now. I am grateful Nathaniel removed you from additional harm."

Priscilla's throat spasmed, and she couldn't breathe. Gasping for air, she jumped up from her chair, holding her neck. Lydia ran to her, striking her on the back with several solid blows. The boulder of bread popped from her mouth, landing behind the chair Lydia vacated.

The reality of everything since her walk on the beach became too much. The tears flowed down her cheeks. "I told him not to leave me. Why did he ever take me in the first place? He hates me. He must." As embarrassed as she knew she should be, she didn't have the strength to combat it. She sobbed like a little girl. Or a broken-hearted woman.

Rushing her, Lydia grasped her elbow. She took her back to Alice's room and walked her to the bed. "I think what you need right now is some additional rest. Lie down. You take a day to revitalize. I'll bring more water later for you to wash up," Lydia suggested.

Hearing the door close, Priscilla crawled in the bed and cried. She let all the emotions she didn't acknowledge over the last weeks flow out of her. All the confusion over her decision to leave home. All the confusion over being taken by Nathaniel, the opposing emotions she felt about him, and the hurt and rejection of him leaving her there, merged in a torrent of pain and doubt.

Not knowing how long she lay on the bed relenting to her recurring tears, she acknowledged her current status. No longer a prisoner, no longer aboard a ship at sea, she could do as she pleased. She didn't have to stay there with his wife. She could do as she wanted. Then again, she knew no one, had no money and limited skills. Currently. She had the ability to change it.

Prying herself from the bed, she inched to the door. She hadn't heard anyone, but she hadn't been listening either. With Nathaniel being a pirate, there must be something of value on site. Gently she pulled the door open. Moving her face forward, she scanned the room. Two light-haired toddlers sat on the floor in the open front door playing.

The boy noticed her and smiled. He poked his playmate, who turned and stared at Priscilla. She had the same face as him. Twins.

The girl stood, stumbling over to Priscilla with her arms in the air. "Up. Up, pweaze," she requested.

Lacking any experience with small children, Priscilla just gawked at her. The child had huge blue eyes like Alice. Were these children Lydia's? And Nathaniel's? None of them inherited Nathaniel's gold eyes.

Alice hurried through the front door. She scolded, "I told you if you don't sit where I can see you, you will have to come back outside." She grabbed the little girl's hand.

Lowering her chin to her chest, the little girl sulked and shuffled along behind Alice. "I sorry. She my friend," she whined, pointing her finger at Priscilla.

"I know, Hannah. Everyone is your friend." Positioning the girl back where she started, Alice rubbed her head. "How can anyone not want to be your friend?" Directing her attention to the boy, she added, "You too, Joseph." The boy giggled and clapped.

"Mother told me you were resting today. What are you doing up?" Alice asked Priscilla.

Witnessing the interaction between the three young individuals provided an unparalleled peace in Priscilla. They were beautiful. "I… uh, I don't feel like it. Are they your brother and sister?"

"Yes. This is Hannah and Joseph."

"They are precious. Like you, Alice." It appeared that Nathaniel and Lydia were a family. With four children. Priscilla knew she didn't belong here. "Your mother and Nathaniel have the four of you then? Henry, and the three of you?"

Several emotions flitted and vacated Alice's eyes before she responded. Confusion. Sadness. A defeated voice replaced her previous chipper one. "There are four of us children." Squatting in front of the toddlers, she suggested, "Let us go on outside. Miss Priscilla can rest."

The little ones did as they were told. They went with Alice outside. She heard Alice singing to them and she realized how happy they appeared. Unlike the memories of her childhood.

Priscilla knew one thing for certain she made the right decision in leaving her mother, and Charles Town. Everything else made no sense, and at that moment, she couldn't begin to attempt to figure it out. She couldn't steal from them and leave. Where would she go? She must make the best of things. First, and foremost, forging whatever form of friendship she could with Lydia. As ridiculous as that notion was, Lydia didn't ask to be in the situation any more than she did.

She had no one. At one time being alone appealed to her. Now it terrified her. Nathaniel would be back. Eventually. She would decide then what she wanted to do, what she needed to do.

Chapter 6

Priscilla managed to get out of bed each morning at daybreak as the others in the household, but that became the extent of her molding herself into her temporary residence. She made the decision to have Nathaniel return her to a port with an English presence. She could make her way from there.

Yes. Nathaniel would know of a location more conducive for an English woman desiring to making it on her own. She preferred living under the protection and company of gentlemen, not savages. But were these fanciful notions? Could a woman have both, on her own and in that region?

The past few days, she helped Lydia and Alice in the kitchen, as little as possible, then she remained indoors. She washed and stored the gathered eggs and any produce they retrieved. She cleaned items used in the morning for making the day's meals and waited for the twins to awaken. Nothing she attempted to do out on the farm resulted in anything other than chaos. And a very flustered Lydia.

The chickens flapped and squawked each time she set foot in their cage. It unnerved her and she flailed about in a frenzied jig. Lydia screeched at her to remain still. She couldn't. Her clothes ended up filthy and ripped the couple of times she went in their pen. Frustrated, Lydia ordered her to stay out of it. She complained about the loss of eggs Priscilla either dropped or that fell from her basket with her hysterics, or the lack of time they had for needless mending.

Priscilla's fondness for the twins deepened each day. Sure, she imagined a child, maybe two in her future, but she believed she would be a mother like hers. You are what you know. Distant, demanding, unyielding. It surprised her how much joy she found in her time with Joseph and Hannah. Their smiles, laughter and play filled her heart with a love she never imagined. She wondered if she had siblings if the emotions wouldn't be so foreign to her.

Dawdling inside the house each morning until Lydia sent Alice to fetch the toddlers became her favorite time of the day. The simplest of tasks, such as assisting with their tiny shoes always turned into tickles and giggles.

With a book in her apron, Priscilla decided to escort them out on the farm leaving them with their mother. She and Alice planned to enjoy the pleasant breeze of the day. Escaping beyond the fence to the shade of a tree, she opened the book and waited on Alice. Normally they read in the evenings, and Alice's reading skills were noticeably improving. She just needed someone to take a little time with her, but Priscilla didn't fault Lydia. She worked from sunup until sundown. The two women engaged with each other seldom. Probably for the best. What would the two discuss with one another without resentment and hostility emerging?

"What are you doing?" Lydia asked, delivering the question in a demeaning and accusatory manner.

Expecting Alice and not Lydia, Priscilla didn't bother to stand. Turning her head meeting Lydia's angry glare, she goaded, "I believe my activity is apparent."

Punching her hands around her waist, Lydia stomped her foot. "Surely you mean your *lack* of activity. I understand a working life is a new concept for you, but with Henry gone I have had to assume his chores. I refuse to work as I do while you take advantage of my hospitality without any contribution!"

"Without any contribution! That's just nonsense! I clean, dress, and assist with your children, and devote time each day to ensure that Alice can read as any woman should." Drawing her knees up, she stood and stuck her finger in Lydia's face. "I don't wish to be here anymore than you wish me to be, but I am attempting to make the best of a very unpleasant situation."

Reaching out her dirty fingers, Lydia gripped Priscilla's bodice yanking her off balance. "Unpleasant situation! You have no idea how unpleasant it could be." Lydia didn't release her and didn't wait for Priscilla to regain her footing. She tugged on the material again pulling Priscilla's face in front of hers. "If you don't cease your ungrateful behavior and take on some of the daily tasks, I will send you away from here!"

As stoic and bold as Priscilla wanted to be, she couldn't. Hearing Lydia threaten to send her away petrified her. She needed to wait for Nathaniel. Get his input and possible passage on his ship. She tried convincing herself seeing him again didn't factor into her reasoning—it did. She couldn't forget the intimacy they shared. His touch. The way he looked at her. And the instances of tenderness and concern.

Lydia's fingers relaxed and fell away from her. Neither woman spoke a word.

Alice's screams from the farm shattered the moment of silence and reflection. She screamed for her mother. Both women ran in that direction. Racing out of the trees, they passed several fleeing men and women from the nearby residences hurrying to return home. Reaching the clearing to the farm, Priscilla halted noticing several men on horseback destroying pens and structures with their enormous swords.

Lydia didn't stop. She rushed right past them toward the front of home.

Hearing Alice's screams again and the cries of the toddlers, Priscilla resumed running. Darting around the horses and the men on foot, she met up with Lydia and Alice at the well in the center of the property. A midnight-haired, black- bearded man sat atop a gold adorned, giant black horse. He spoke to Lydia in a language unfamiliar to Priscilla. It shocked her to hear Lydia respond, speaking foreign words.

Priscilla didn't see the twins. Lydia and the man shared a few more exchanges before a large man strode out the front door of the house with a toddler dangling from each hand. He held each upside down by a foot.

Hannah wailed.

Joseph didn't seem to be able to draw a breath. He wheezed.

Lydia fell to her knees beside the horse of the man she conversed with. Screaming, she clasped her hands in front of her.

Priscilla experienced her panic and pain. She darted toward the man with the children.

Lydia yelled at her. "Don't! Stop!"

Stepping on the bottom step, he tossed Hannah. She hit the ground to Priscilla's left in a thud that reverberated through every pore in her body. Hannah's wails stopped. Hurrying to her, Priscilla knelt and picked up her limp body. Her eyes were wide and stared into Priscilla's, but only hisses of air came from her chest.

Lydia pleaded behind her in the odd language. Priscilla pulled Hannah's body to her, rubbing her back. After what seemed an eternity of terror, the young girl coughed then wailed again. Cradling her, Priscilla sat on the ground, using her body to shield the tiny one.

Keeping her head lowered against the top of Hannah's head, she didn't look to see the destruction taking place around her, but she heard it. Chickens squawked. She smelled fire and heard wood cracking.

Lydia continued to communicate with the intruders. What started as appeals transformed into resistances. Her voice grew louder and turned harder.

The sound of heavy boots and the quiet sobs of Joseph alerted Priscilla that the heartless, dangerous man walked near her. Hugging Hannah tightly to her, she couldn't bring herself to look. It horrified her imagining what he may do to her, or worse, to the children.

Lydia shrieked. Joseph howled in fright. Priscilla couldn't disregard them and turned her head to the scene behind her. The man on horseback held the small boy against his chest, a knife against his tear-stricken pale face. He yelled at Lydia. She shook her head returning his determined words with her own.

Squeezing Hannah close to her, Priscilla viewed the heated exchange between them. She watched as he drew his blade down the side of Joseph's face leaving a trail of blood.

Joseph's wails of anguish drowned every other sound. Blood oozed from the cut pooling in the neck of his shirt.

"Yes. Yes," yelled Lydia before reverting back to the tormentor's language. The dark-eyed man nodded at her before shoving the boy in her direction. Lydia's quick, frenzied steps had her beside the huge animal before Joseph hit the dirt. "Alice! Take him into the house. Apply pressure to his wound," she directed. Lydia pried his arms from around her neck passing him off to Alice's trembling arms. "Do as I said. It will be over soon," she insisted. Stepping in front of the horse, she walked towards the trees.

The wicked man urged his horse to follow her. Most of the other men did the same.

Jumping up with Hannah, Priscilla raced to the house ushering in Alice and Joseph. Sitting him on the table, Alice placed a cloth in a bowl and filled it with water. Lifting the cloth, she attempted several times to apply it to Joseph's face, but he wailed and twisted from her. "Priscilla, put her down and hold him for me." Alice requested. Her voice shaking.

He had been through enough. Priscilla couldn't fathom restraining him. "I can't," she whimpered.

Raising her voice, Alice insisted, "You have to! The wound is wide and deep. It will need to be sewn." Begging Priscilla with her eyes, she promised, "He won't remember. It's for his own good."

Lowering Hannah to the floor, the girl grasped Priscilla's leg wrapping herself around it. Alice managed to get Joseph laid back on the table. Priscilla placed a hand on each of his shoulders, holding him still while Alice washed and applied pressure to his cheek. His cries lessened as his older sister sang songs to him. Before long, his eyes closed and he appeared to sleep.

Looking down Priscilla saw Hannah wrapped up in her skirt. She also appeared to be asleep. "What happened out there? Who were those men? Where's your mother?" whispered Priscilla to Alice.

"Spanish. We hear that the battles between the French and the Spanish here on Tortuga have increased, but being inland, we have been spared." Alice continued holding the cloth to her brother's face. Priscilla admired her strength and calm. She had seen and endured much for such a young girl. For anyone. "I don't know about my mother. I only understood a few words between them."

Alice lived a life much different than the one Priscilla had ever known. She felt ashamed that a twelve-year old possessed necessary qualities in difficult situations and she didn't. "Your mother will return soon. I am sure of it." Her determination grew. She wouldn't be the weak woman that depended on a girl to guide her. She would be a better woman. She admired Lydia's fortitude in the wake of an enemy and her dedication to her children.

The clattering of the farm under destruction grew louder since the children quieted and the gravity of the raid bore down on them. Through the window smoke billowed from the burning of the wrecked outbuildings. Down the front path she saw the meager fields on fire. Afraid to move, afraid to go outside, they stood beside the wooden table with the sleeping children, watching the wreckage of their livelihood.

The door flew open and a frantic Lydia bustled in. "Come. Now. They are setting the house on fire," she said in a calm tone betrayed by the anxious look in her eyes. "Follow me to the wagon."

Priscilla picked up Hannah and Lydia scooped up Joseph pressing his head to her chest with the cloth between them. They ran down the steps towards the stable, what remained of the stable. The wagon sat alongside it as it had since Priscilla arrived. But the barn burned. Placing Joseph in the back, Lydia scanned every direction before instructing Alice. "Over there! In the trees behind the chickens… Charlie. Go get him Alice."

Alice did as her mom directed.

Not knowing anything about any 'Charlie', Priscilla looked where Alice sped off to. Just inside the trees, she saw a mule. Alice retrieved him, pulling him behind her back to the wagon. He reared a few times, but she had a good hold on his reins.

Gripping Priscilla's hand, Lydia placed it on the cloth over Joseph's wound. Priscilla placed Hannah beside him in the wagon. Lydia went to the front of the wagon and she and Alice hitched it to Charlie.

"Get in the back with your brother." Climbing up on the seat, Lydia turned and yelled, "Everyone in!" Priscilla jumped in after Alice. The wagon lurched and they headed away from the house. Away from the farm. The smells and sounds of such cruel acts taken on women and children would haunt Priscilla forever.

Joseph whimpered throughout the bumpy ride. Priscilla situated herself with his head in her lap doing her best to hinder his bleeding, but it saturated the cloth. They passed several people during the ride, but no one spoke to them. Priscilla wondered if Lydia rode with any particular destination in mind. She forged relationships with her neighbors, why didn't they turn to them?

Late afternoon, the ocean came into view. Lydia headed toward the town Nathaniel brought Priscilla through just a few days ago. Could Nathaniel still be here? Had he been in town with his whore? Why did Lydia let him treat her so? First, bringing Priscilla to their home and dumping her off, then the knowledge that he visited, and most likely paid a woman in town?

Without any alternate plans to suggest, Priscilla remained silent. Lydia directed the wagon through town, down the narrow road, pulling in between two buildings. One being the brothel. It stunk. It smelled of ale, rum, human excrement, and vomit.

Having ripped off a section of her skirt on the ride, she pulled the ends around Joseph's head tying them together. Bounding off the wagon she confronted Lydia as she stepped to the ground. "We don't need him. You can't. You won't," she challenged.

Lydia shoved her aside. "Get out of my way. I am here for Joseph. You make no sense."

A sultry, foreign accent cooed. "Ah, Madame Fuller, I have been expecting you. I heard talk this evening of inland farms burned by the Spaniards." The woman stood in an archway leading to the whorehouse. Her large breasts were confined in a bodice tied too tight and they rested close to her chin. Even in the dim lighting one could not disregard the prominent red stain over her lips.

Moving to the back of the wagon, Lydia assisted Alice and Hannah to the ground. "I have nowhere else to go, Sabine. Joseph is wounded. He needs a doctor."

The woman's black ringlets framing her face bounced as she made way to Joseph and scrutinized his condition. "Master Davies did not call upon me his last return, gave me nothing to add to my purse, Madame," she stated.

Though not much shorter in stature than the French woman, Lydia straightened her back and stepped up to her. "He had to leave in a rush. You know he is an honest man. He will repay his debt."

Turning her gaze to Priscilla, Sabine smirked. "I has heard of him parting with Archer. Tsk. Tsk. He just can't seem to keep any allies. He is digging his own grave. *Oui*?" Stepping around Lydia, she came to Priscilla taking her chin in her hand and turning her face from side to side. "*Belle femme* indeed. This face will pay any debt. Master Davies did leave me a *cadeau*... a..." Flipping her free hand palm up, she bounced it in the air, puckering her lips searching for her translation. "A gift."

"Not now, Sabine! Get Joseph to a doctor," argued Lydia.

Releasing Priscilla, Sabine raised her arm in the air snapping her fingers. "*Marguerite, allez*." A young woman appeared from the archway with her head lowered. Sabine instructed, "Take Madame and the boy to Raoul."

The young woman waited while Lydia gathered Joseph in

her arms. Lydia turned to Priscilla and directed, "Come on. Stay with Alice and Hannah."

Priscilla lifted Hannah into her arms. They followed the woman through the archway and up a narrow staircase to the left. The profanity, moaning, and groaning on the other side of the doors they passed shocked Priscilla. A couple of men opened doors they walked by in various stages of redressing. Her stomach rolled imagining Nathaniel partaking in these activities. Leaving the hallway, they entered an open aired walkway attaching the building to another behind it. Joseph whimpered and fidgeted in Lydia's arms, and she did her best to soothe him.

Inside the other building, the young woman stopped in front of a door. A woman's cries came from the other side. Knocking lightly, she announced, "Raoul, it's Marguerite. Madame Sabine requested I seek you…"

A tall, gray-haired man snatched the door open. Behind him, a crying woman pushed down her skirt and moved off of a dirty wooden table. "Marguerite, Madame Sabine mentioned only Delphine and Margaux," he stated. She moved aside allowing Lydia to step forward.

"Sir, my son received a cut on his face. Our home burned to the ground. I have nothing. Nothing to clean it or stitch it." Lydia marched right into the room placing Joseph on the unsanitary table. "Sabine offered your services. Please."

Snatching the arm of the woman he assisted prior, he grumbled, "*Margaux, aller*. Go. Get." He shoved her through the door. Noticing Priscilla, Hannah and Alice, he asked, "Just the boy? Correct?"

Joseph began crying, Lydia's impatience mounted. "Yes, just him. Hurry."

The door slammed cutting them off from Lydia and Joseph. Priscilla, Hannah and Alice waited. With nowhere else to go, they had to endure the screams of the poor boy as the doctor treated and sewed his face.

When his cries subsided, the two women sat on the floor and breathed easier. Hannah slept in Priscilla's arms. Priscilla herself must have dozed, as Sabine startled her. "Mademoiselles, I trust Raoul is about finished... no?" Cracking the door, she and Raoul spoke a few words to each other in French before she closed it again. "He is inspecting his work. The boy will scar, but scars are proof of surviving a tragedy. A symbol of force... um, strength."

Handing Hannah to Alice, Priscilla rose to her feet. Standing so close to Sabine, and in the lit hallway, she saw the scars her face and neck bore. Though she wore her hair to hide most of it, one could still see she had her throat cut from ear to ear in the past. Shifting her focus to Sabine's eyes, she asked, "Is Nathaniel here?"

Sabine's right eyebrow lifted, she whispered her response, "Nathaniel? Master Davies allows you to call him by his father's name? You have cast a spell on him, Mademoiselle. I only know of Madame Fuller ever addressing him as such." She chuckled. "Without gaining a mangled face anyway."

The longer she stayed here the less she realized she knew of him. "Is he not here?"

Sabine's red lips turned up in a knowing smile. "You don't know him the way you wish. Master Davies spends little time at my establishment but is generous when he does."

Sabine's comment wasn't a statement or a question. Truth being, Priscilla didn't know him. Raoul opened the door, and Lydia came out holding a sleeping Joseph. Halting, Lydia cupped her hand on Raoul's shoulder. "I will repay your generosity."

He looked to Sabine, then back to Lydia. He patted her hand and nodded.

After the traumatic events of the day, the noise of the bar

and brothel didn't hinder sleep for any of them. Sabine had prepared a room through the main courtyard on the backside of the building for them. Lydia seemed familiar and comfortable with the space. She took the bed with her children, and Sabine had a couple of makeshift beds brought in and set up on the floor. Priscilla took one and didn't wake until possibly midday the next day.

The three children slept on the bed still, but she didn't see Lydia. Cracking the door, she didn't locate her, but she saw several individuals roaming about. They looked to be workers, carrying bags filled with produce. Others carried baskets of linens. She hesitated before venturing out of the room and leaving the children, but she needed to know that Lydia was there, and safe.

Rounding the corner entry to the courtyard, she glimpsed Sabine's back. She sat leaning over a table, appearing to be in a private, serious conversation with another individual. Her black hair cascaded down her back in dark ringlets. Several local people cleaned the area and carried out broken chairs and tables. As she walked closer to Sabine, she realized Lydia sat across the table. She hid her hair and much of her face under a silk scarf. Her eyes widened as Priscilla approached.

"Are the children all right?" she asked, jumping out of her chair, her concern evident.

"Yes… yes, they are still sleeping. I wanted to know that you are safe. I am sorry to alarm you, and I am sorry if I interrupted." Switching her focus to Sabine, the hair on her arms stood on end noticing the devious smirk and unsettling glint in her eyes.

"No interruption at all, Mademoiselle. Please, grab a chair and sit with us." Waving her arm toward a chair a few feet away, Priscilla observed the numerous gold bracelets adorning her wrist and lower arm. "Madame Fuller and I were discussing the payment for my generosity."

This woman expected payment for coming to the aid of women and children who lost everything. And one of the children required medical assistance? Certainly, Lydia couldn't be considering staying? Not that they had anywhere else to go, but why would they stay in such an establishment and what sort of payment could they offer when they didn't have anything. "I believe that is a private conversation," Priscilla responded, making no attempt to join them. "I will return to the children."

Throwing up her skirts, revealing quite more besides her black stockings than Priscilla wished to see, Sabine kicked the chair nearest to her closer to Priscilla. "It wasn't a request, Mademoiselle. Madame Fuller and I have an ongoing arrangement. It doesn't include les enfants nor yourself." Spreading her legs and planting her feet on the ground, she crossed her arms under her bosom, lifting it. She tapped one of her fingers against her red lips. "Then again, the one *fille* is close to years when you came to me," she emphasized, pinning Lydia with an unsavory stare.

The threat and the reality of the words given their current situation and location caused a shiver starting in Priscilla's toes migrating up her entire body. True concern and pure rage surged her simultaneously. She couldn't be referring to Alice? "Alice is but a child. How could you mention something so cruel... so vulgar?" Priscilla challenged.

Sabine's face hardened. Her glare exhibited such ferocity Priscilla feared it singed her skin and hair. "*Vous ne savez rien!*" Sabine shouted. Slamming her hands on her knees, she leaned forward, snarling her words, "You know nothing... nothing about cruelty and vulgarity. And as I expected, you will work in her stead." She slapped her hands on the table and stood. Eyeing both women, she fixed a scowl on Lydia first, waving her away from the table, "*Poursuivre.* Get. *Tes bebes* will expect to eat...*oui?*"

After several stalled attempts to stand only to return to her seat, Lydia stretched her torso across the table and cautioned in a low voice, "Priscilla was left in my care by Nathaniel. You, as well as I know not to cross him, Sabine."

A drunken man passed out across a table in a far corner Priscilla didn't notice before, lifted his head and belched before collapsing where he started. Sabine laughed. Not at the patron, but more at Lydia. "Madame Fuller, why would you think I would want to do anything to upset Monsieur Davies. I am but a businesswoman, *tu ne crois pas*? You have delivered me a product that will provide us all with a great profit. If, and when he returns, your debts will be paid and you can take leave wherever you desire, *mon amie*."

An understanding, relief and acceptance appeared and rested in Lydia's features. She nodded and left the table.

Priscilla stared at her retreating back unsure of anything. Should she follow? What agreement did the two women just make, and what exact role did she have?

An arm came around her back and wrapped around her shoulders startling her. Sabine drew Priscilla's ear toward her mouth and coaxed, "You and I will be the greatest of friends, you will see." She fingered the blonde strands of hair at Priscilla's temple. "With this crown of yours and that face... all the foolish men will hand over the riches. All will come to Sabine's at a chance to have this *belle*." Taking Priscilla's elbow, she led her to the room she shared with Lydia and the children. "Rest and eat. Margaux will come for you when it is time." She stepped away from the door leaving Priscilla staring at it blankly before stating, "Priscilla, *ma belle*, your introduction this evening will be one to rejoice."

Chapter 7

Nathaniel, Henry and their small crew accepted their meager earnings from the captain of the Lady Island and trudged along the pier. They were tired. They were frustrated on so many levels. Joining the crew of the Lady Island served their purpose. They assisted in a couple small raids to and from Port Royal, but the prize promised to him by Archer wasn't the ship he remembered.

Archer stripped the Intrepid leaving nothing but a hull in need of costly and timely repair. They careened it and started its restoration, but it required much more than Nathaniel expected. James and Matthew stayed behind to continue, and Nathaniel enlisted a group of men he met at a port tavern. He wished they had come upon a good battle on the return sail. As much as his wrath for Archer consumed and fueled him, he had himself to blame as well. And that blonde, blue-eyed beauty he couldn't resist and possessed his every waking and sleeping thought.

They didn't make it far off the docks before news of the Spaniards attack on several inland farms reached their ears.

He attempted to appear unaffected by this information as Henry walked beside him and he didn't want to alarm him.

His impassive facade failed him. The drunken boastings from men they passed defeated him. They crowed of how the spent all their wages and would again for a night with the white-haired beauty from the colonies.

Grabbing one of the braggarts by the throat, Nathaniel forced him to his back in the dirt. "Where is this woman you speak of?" he demanded.

"Sa…Sabine's," the man replied, his hands up by his ears signifying his concession. "You can have her too, but you'll have to wait. She entertains but one man per evening, and Sabine had to start a roster. I have even heard before you get your name on it she is forcing payment."

Nathaniel kicked the man in the side hard enough he rolled over and retched. He yearned to continue the assault. It couldn't be Priscilla they spoke of? She wouldn't do such things. A lady. Not his clean, unblemished, beautiful Angel.

"Nathaniel. We need to check on Ma…Alice, the twins," yelled Henry.

Reaching for a mug of rum on the table he pulled the man from, Nathaniel downed it. He finished the others remaining in front of the men standing at the table watching the entire scene with half-smirks on their faces. Throwing the final one he drained and pinning one of the grinning idiots in the forehead, he flung his arm behind him swiping the empties across the table before marching off toward Sabine's.

He didn't hear anything. He didn't see anything. He had only one focus—Priscilla. How dare she give away something of his. How dare she disrespect him. He had enough of that at sea. He certainly didn't need it from her. Some lady she turned out to be. She had an ass-whooping and a hard-fucking due like she never knew possible.

Storming into Sabine's, his heart pounded in his ears, as

did the rush of his blood coursing through his veins. Men with 'ladies' filled every seat. Some were dancing. Many had their heads back chugging on their drinks or engaged in boisterous laughter. Yet he heard none of it. He scanned the space but didn't see Priscilla, nor Sabine. "Priscilla! If you're in here, you better present yourself now." he hollered.

All eyes shot to him. All movement halted. Still Priscilla didn't appear. Jacob, one of his crew, pushed a mug into his hand. Nathaniel drank it and held it out for more. Without hesitation, Jacob refilled it.

"Cap'n, I thought you wanted us to keep unnoticed as best we could manage. Get a woman, keep out of sight, then depart in the morn. Has that changed?" Jacob probed, anticipation evident in his wide eyes and the darting of his tongue between the large void of missing teeth in his eager smile.

Once again, Nathaniel realized he did indeed act on emotion. Archer preached this to him for years. And Hackett beat him mercilessly because of it. He had risen above that. Yes, he had. Until her. This would cost her dearly. "Nothing has changed. Take one and enjoy her," Nathaniel directed.

Redirecting his focus, he looked upon Henry. He wanted Henry to have every opportunity to be a fortunate man with a reputation of pride. It disgusted him that he, himself displayed so little in front of the boy he swore to provide such. How could he have Henry emulate him when he failed him?

Lydia. How could he not give her a moment's thought? "Come, Henry," he stated. Walking through the maze of people he led them through the courtyard separating the tavern, the kitchen, and the servant quarters. It involved rejecting several women's advances and lugging Henry out of their clutches. If Lydia had to leave the farm, he knew where to find her. The exact place, the only location, he managed to acquire eighteen years ago. Perhaps not ideal, but it provided success in the most crucial endeavor of his life. Preserving the safety and anonymity of Lydia and her unborn child.

As he hoped and handsomely compensated Sabine for, Jean-Paul stopped them before they entered the hallway. If anything, Sabine managed and operated a rather regulated business More than most in her profession. Jean-Paul, a colored, tower of a man, glowered at Nathaniel before grumbling in his deep, chesty voice, "You are not one to usually cause such a commotion, Master Davies. Please assure me that it was but an isolated incident and has concluded."

Nathaniel respected Jean-Paul. Obviously, an educated man besides an intimidating one.

Nathaniel nodded. "I wish to speak with Miss Fowler. She is back here is she not?"

Jean-Paul's arms relaxed from across his broad torso, falling to his sides. He made no attempt to move his barrel of a body out of their path though. "Indeed she is. With the young ones. No trouble."

"No trouble," Nathaniel repeated. "I have her older boy with me. He wishes to see her as well."

Taking a deep breath and releasing it, Jean-Paul stepped out of their way. Not since Henry's birth had Nathaniel walked down that corridor. He had been younger than Henry himself at that time. Out of so much tragedy, he managed Lydia's escape from Hackett. Until then, he provided and made it possible for her to have the simple life she longed for. Safety. Children.

Knowing she waited behind the door disgusted him. He swore to protect her, always. He failed. He rested his forehead on the wood stalling his entry. Because of more loss and misfortune, he once again came to the door they hid her behind, the one she gave birth in all those years ago. It pained him more than it did the first time

Tapping lightly on the door, an influx of peace and gratefulness overcame him as soon as it cracked open and Lydia's familiar eyes changed from alarm to joy. Throwing the door wide, she jumped into him, her arms around his neck. "This wait has been the worst." Releasing Nathaniel, she jumped away from him and sobbed, "Henry...come here." She held her arms open and he rushed into them.

"Ma...ma, stop, stop. I'm well," Henry laughed. Her hands were everywhere. She touched and turned his face, his head, his neck, and he gripped her hands stopping her examination as she tugged his shirt up revealing his stomach. "I return without a mark on me. Besides the ones I left with that is."

"Henry. Nathaniel. You returned," Alice squealed. Her youthful face appeared from under the small section of lightweight bedcover covering only her head.

"Shh, you'll wake--," scolded Lydia, but too late. Joseph bounced up from a dead sleep and scooted off the bed throwing his arms around Henry's legs.

Hannah rubbed her eyes with her tiny fists. "You did come back 'Enry. And 'Thaniel." She spread her arms wide for a hug, tilted her head grinning and waited on them to come to her.

Nathaniel went to her lifted her from the bed and squeezed her tight. "Always, little girl, always." They had much they needed to discuss, much he didn't want to with the children present and awake. "You are all satisfactory? Priscilla too?"

His inquiry disrupted their jubilant reunion. Lydia's back stiffened. She looked to him with sorrow and trepidation. "Yes. We lost the farm," she muttered.

He realized she had more unfavorable details to divulge. She verified what he already suspected. A blonde beauty could now be found at Sabine's. And Lydia, Priscilla and the children were there because they had nowhere else to go.

They were alive. They did what they must. Removing Lydia and the children from there were his priority.

He tried to tell himself it applied to Priscilla as well, but no woman of his could give herself to another man. She didn't have need to. What she did from that point forward mattered little to him. But his mind and his heart couldn't acknowledge such a limited sentiment. He held little faith of sustaining it.

The next revelation came slow, but it came. And it changed everything. "The chest. The chest, Lydia. They didn't get the chest, right?" he thundered. Shifting Hannah back onto the bed, he glared at Lydia fisted his hands repeatedly. He had not and would never hurt her, but the fury swelled and threatened to breach. "Did you leave it at the farm? Tell me you left it there. Tell me——," he raged.

Biting her lower lip, her eyes filled with tears. She stuttered, "I ha…had to. They hurt Hannah. He. He cut Joseph." She reached for Nathaniel's wrist, but he sidestepped her. "I'm sorry. He knew. Somehow, he knew. Hackett. It had to be Hackett."

The children started crying. Lydia remained strong and resilient for those children, even when Patrick died. Seeing her upset distressed them. She made a valid point. The Spaniards had information. Information valuable enough for them to risk coming to this area and implementing a raid. He couldn't think. He needed to leave before he made a huge mistake. Shaking his head, as if that could sort his thoughts and emotions and aid him in formulating some semblance of an alternate plan, he strutted to the door. "I will see you in the morning." He wanted rum. He wanted a fight.

He expected to arrive on Tortuga and curb his frustrations over the setback with the Intrepid by drowning himself in rum and sinking himself in Priscilla. He aimed to appease his desire for Priscilla permanently. At least temporarily.

Returning to a homeless family exacerbated an already crucial situation.

He had no ship. He lost the chest with his hoard. Hackett would pursue him. And his thoughts always returned to Priscilla. He couldn't have it. He had too many vital concerns to occupy his mind and drive his efforts.

Sputtering, he flung himself upright in his chair, slinging wetness out of his eyes and hair. "What the hell!" Nathaniel hollered. His head pounded. Lifting a hand to his forehead, he pressed it there scanning his surroundings.

Priscilla stood beside him dangling an empty water pitcher at her side. Every part of him awakened at the sight of her. If possible, she looked more beautiful than he remembered and dreamt of. Even with the anger in her eyes and the venom spewing from her exquisite mouth, he had never laid eyes upon something he wanted as badly as her.

"You are an ass, Nathaniel. A complete and utter ass," she fumed. Heaving the pitcher at his head, he ducked and it crashed into the wall behind him. Shards of it pelted the top of his head and bare shoulders. Slapping her hands on her hips, she paced and circled. Her mouth never stopped. "You take me. You leave me here. With your wife and family. Only to be attacked and forced to come to... to this. And you manage to finally make your way back to take another woman!"

Cecile, one of Sabine's pretty and voluptuous younger girls, interrupted from the far corner where she washed herself. "If you believe it was me he took, you are mistaken, Belle. Master Davies indulged in enough rum to down a large horse. Madame Sabine requested I bring him up here and put him to bed. All he did was carry-on about some Priscilla angel."

He didn't recall any of that, but even so, it didn't give Priscilla any right to come in here, wake him from a sound sleep, and engage him as she did. Grabbing her arm, he pulled her on the bed and over his lap. Good thing he didn't lift her skirt because she needed any extra possible padding she could manage. He had absolutely no self-control remaining. Ever since he saw her, he couldn't think straight. She proved to be more troublesome than he ever imagined. And she earned herself a sound punishment. He spanked her hard and steady.

Cecile shoved her arms into an over garment and ran out of the room.

"I wouldn't have had to seek another woman's attentions if the one I left here waited on my return. Now would I?" he roared continuing his punishment. She bucked, wriggled and kicked. His palm missed its intended target more than contacted it. After a few more wild strikes that landed on her hipbone, upper thigh, even his own leg, he stopped. Lifting his arms behind his head, he leaned back away from her resisting the desire to continue.

Wasting no time, she pressed her palms down, one into his groin region, the other on the bed propelling herself off his thighs. Stumbling, she landed on her bottom. This served to ignite her ire more. "You have no claim to me. You won't. You don't. You never will," she ranted.

Her breasts rose and fell with each outburst. He didn't hear a word. The anger they shared became irrelevant. Lurching toward her, his knees smashing onto the floor, he gripped her behind the neck and crushed his mouth onto hers.

She tasted as sweet as he remembered. She attempted to turn away from him—at first. Soon enough she not only returned his kiss, she matched it. A frenzy of lips, tongues, moans, even teeth ensued. Scrambling to her knees, their mouths never ceasing to taste, lick, and savor wherever they touched, he wrapped one hand around her waist holding her tight to his torso. Splaying his hand in the back of her hair, he tugged her head back and indulged himself in the soft, perfect skin of her neck.

The more aggressive his lavish attention became, the more she responded. Her fingers threaded in his hair, clenching. Her chin dropped and tiny, sweet pants sounded. Scooping her up, he placed her on the bed. His hands roamed over her shoulders, sliding her garment lower, revealing her breasts. Cupping each one, he sucked them until her legs wrapped around his waist and her hands clawed at him for more.

And he intended to give her what she wanted. He freed her hips and legs of her garment and rid himself of his pants.

The first thrust nearly did him in. Stalling, he gazed at her beneath him. So very beautiful. Observing her desire, her eagerness in her expression and in her body's acceptance, he feared making a move. He didn't want it to end before it got started. Her breathing came fast. Her eyes were wide, yet serenely blissful.

Placing a finger on her lips, he ran it across the lower one. The heat in her gasps fanned his palm. Her tongue contacted his fingertip. She stroked it lightly before moving to the next one. He watched her with fascination and patience. He didn't want to miss a mere second of the experience. He wanted to savor every single and shared sensation.

Withdrawing slowly, he eased back deep inside her before repeating the torturous pleasure. Her eyelids fluttered, but she continued attending to his fingertips with her tongue and lips. The bliss in her face and the soft mews reflected the extreme heightened arousal he too existed in.

The quivering of her thighs on his hips, the glistening of her skin, and her taut nipples held and suspended him in an existence he never shared with another woman. He didn't want it to end. He wanted to be the only man to ever see and engage in it with her. He didn't want to share it with anyone else—only her.

A pulse in her core squeezed him. He stilled, anticipating the next. It occurred. Stronger than the first. Grasping under her thigh with his free hand, he lifted and tilted her. Delivering a couple of quick, small pumps, he slid all the way in, giving her all of him. Her body tremored. Her head jerked back. Her chin snapped up. Her hands grasped and clenched the bed linens. She came hard, moaning and writhing. Nothing could be as stunning as she.

With his other hand freed from her exquisite lips, he gripped her other thigh. He started and maintained a fixed rhythm until she peaked again. He joined her.

Resting his torso on her, he remained kneeling by the bed basking in the satisfaction he found and had with her. Both breathed heavily.

He hoped to ignore everything that awaited him, but she decided she needed to clear her conscience.

"Nathaniel. Nathaniel, I did wait on you. No other man has taken me," she confessed.

Closing his eyes, her admission pleased him, and he wished it didn't. The desire to be the man she not only wanted, but needed, consumed him. It could never be. Since that day he saw her on the beach he betrayed too many. Mainly, himself.

In her presence, he lost all good sense. He abandoned his ambitions. That, as well as she, were both unacceptable.

Strikes to his head snapped him out of his reverie. Swat after swat came at his head. Fingernails dug into his shoulders as she slapped and pushed for him to move.

"What the hell is wrong with you now, woman?" he challenged.

Shooting upright, her feet kicked him in the chest and stomach as she scooted away from him and off the bed.

"I hate you, Nathaniel. I truly do. Even with you deserting me with your family for some absurd reason, I wanted you to know I didn't share with another man what you and I have—and just did. And you say nothing. Nothing!" Adjusting her garment up over her breasts, she threw her hands and face to the heavens. "Why? Why am I such a foolish woman?"

"Stop behaving as some misunderstood child. Do you honestly think Sabine didn't inform me of your duplicitous arrangement soon after my arrival? I don't like other men even entertaining the thought of having you, much less believing they have, but it's better than the alternative." He climbed onto the bed and stretched out. Hands behind his head, ankles crossed. "Of course, she didn't provide me all the compensation details, but I'm certain you have solicited a hefty sum. And honestly, I'm grateful to learn of it as I have need of it." He watched as her eyes traveled the length of his nude body.

Her cheeks heated realizing he observed her admiration. Taking her bottom lip between her teeth, she seemed to think before she spoke—this time. Coolly she expressed, "I have no intention of handing my earnings over to you. Not now. Not ever."

He misinterpreted her, obviously. If she thought, she could do anything, no matter how innocent it happened to be, with her body—she made a huge blunder. Soon enough the ruse she and Sabine orchestrated would become common knowledge. If one man suspected the woman he bedded wasn't the one he paid for, both women would suffer. They were lucky to have escaped exposure to that point. "We're leaving here. All of us. In order to do so, I need your shares." He stated his intentions and closed his eyes signaling the conversation ended and she had no alternative.

Motion to the bed jostled his feet. Cracking one eye, he found her sitting with her back to him on the far edge. Leaning forward, her face in her hands, he didn't hear any, but he saw her body flinch with what he assumed were sobs. He did hate to see a woman cry. "What is it now, Priscilla? You can't expect to stay here. Soon enough your deception will be known. It is better I get you out of Tortuga before that occurs."

Dropping her hands to her sides, she straightened her back and lifted her head. Blonde curls bounced and swayed around her slender waist. "I've done a great many things I regret, and how this most unforgivable one escaped me until now, I will never understand," she professed.

"You're speaking in riddles," Nathaniel stated when she didn't continue.

Twisting her head, she turned her teary eyes to his. "Before... on the ship, I didn't know of Lydia and the children. Now, I do. And I know them. I school Alice every day. How can I go to them now? I have betrayed them." Tears flowed from her sad eyes and down her porcelain cheeks. "I am no better than the woman my patrons believe me to be. I'm actually worse. I had hoped Lydia and I were becoming friends of sorts... finally. Now I'll have no one. As I deserve."

He found it odd she mentioned 'wife' earlier but didn't think much of it. He didn't think much of anything other than having his hands and all of him on her again at that time. The realization that Lydia didn't explain their relationship and history rattled him. Why didn't she?

Seeing and hearing Priscilla's shame and sorrow wounded him. It was unnecessary. Throwing his legs off the bed, he pulled his pants on. Wrapping his fingers around her elbow, he urged, "Get up. Come with me."

She shrugged out of his hold, falling on her side on the

bed. "Don't touch me. That's the last thing I want. If I were a woman of stronger character, I wouldn't be in this position."

Laughter erupted from deep in his chest. He couldn't restrain it. Priscilla had strong character. He had first-hand knowledge of that. If he didn't like her... actually like her, besides being enthralled with her captivating beauty, he would be making the necessary preparations for them to depart. Instead, he felt compelled to ease her conscience. "Priscilla, don't make me put you over my shoulder and march you downstairs. Come along," he urged.

Wiping her hands over her eyes and cheeks, she sat up. "Where are we going?" she asked.

Going to the door, he opened it and stood waiting for her to join him. She stalled longer than he should have allowed, but she followed.

Chapter 8

Sitting on a bench in the courtyard, Priscilla buried her trembling hands under her skirts. She breathed deep and steady. Lydia sat beside her. Nathaniel stood in front of them, stationary except for a slight twist to his head as he prompted and mediated their exchange.

They weren't married. Nathaniel and Lydia had never been in a physical relationship, and the children weren't his. That's the information Priscilla learned thus far.

"But why did you never correct me, Lydia? You never said anything to make me believe otherwise. All these weeks I assumed you disliked me because you were his wife and he and I dishonored you . What other reason have I given you?" implored Priscilla.

Lydia's eyes challenged Nathaniel. She stared at him intently. "You should have come to me first. Alone. To discuss this," Lydia contended.

Narrowing his eyes, Nathaniel replied, "Don't lecture me, Lydia. Not now. Patrick is not here. You and the children are under my care now. We are departing together, and I won't sail with two women who don't share and understand the complete severity of all it entails. You both will need to trust and depend on one another."

Jumping up to stand in front of him, Lydia fumed, "And what have we been doing? We all seemed to be alive and thriving before you returned and decided you needed to force all the truths be laid out."

Poking her in the chest with his finger until she returned to her seat, he cautioned, "Sit back down. Out on the open sea no one thrives without loyalty… solidarity. I can't manage what I need to if I can't rely on you two to follow instructions and work together."

"She doesn't belong here. I know it. You know it. I hoped you would return her sooner than later, not keep her. The less she knows, the easier it would have been for her. Her heart, Nathaniel. Let her believe you are just another heartless, thieving pirate. But no. By you having me do this the damage will be greater for her when you do eventually leave her. And you will. It's who you are. Who've you become," declared Lydia.

The realization and guilt in Nathaniel's face supported Lydia's assertion as truth. He swallowed hard. "I'll be handling our departure. It will be two days." His gaze found Priscilla's. They revealed regret and apology. "I need your earnings to finance it. Just give them to me without argument. And no returning upstairs. As long as I am seeing to your safety and needs, it won't be necessary. If I discover you have defied my demands, you will be punished." Gripping her shoulder, tighter than necessary, he directed her off the bench. "Go get your pieces and bring them to me."

Her thoughts went in so many directions. As did her emotions. She couldn't distinguish what she wanted and what she didn't, any longer. Between the moments, she accepted her fate and decided to find and hold onto what pleasure she could derive from it, from the moments she experienced extreme loneliness, to the rare ones she found the utmost happiness in Nathaniel's presence, the one certainty she knew without a doubt—she had none.

For a brief instance, she experienced relief learning that Nathaniel and Lydia were not married. But why? It's not as if he cared or asked what she wanted or what she expected. Not once. When he tired of her, he would abandon her.

Retrieving her purse, she shoved it into Nathaniel's hands. She made a decent profit. It didn't bother her that he demanded she give it to him. She hadn't considered how or on what she would spend it, other than assisting Lydia and the children in acquiring a new residence. It seemed Nathaniel shouldered that responsibility.

What did Priscilla think would happen? Evidently, she didn't think about much in the weeks since the attack. She didn't think at all. Believing he, Lydia and the children were a family, what role did she expect to have? She had no expectations other than surviving. She did what she must and didn't allow herself the luxury of questioning it or judging it.

Nathaniel's hands covered hers. He didn't remove them. Staring at the ground, she couldn't bring herself to look at him. With his return and disrupting the routine she made for herself, she would have time to reflect on all that occurred, all she engaged in and what her future may entail.

The reality of it all squeezed her stomach so tight she struggled to remain where she stood and not locate a bucket to expel its contents.

"Angel, I will make it right. Lydia is correct. You don't belong here," he expressed in a voice so low she barely heard him. Placing a finger under her chin, he lifted her face. He looked as solemn as she felt. If these declarations hurt him as much as they did her, then why execute them? Lowering his head, his lips came to hers. He held them there. His breath passed between them merging with hers.

Inhaling him as far and deep as she could, as if for the last time, she gasped. Tearing her mouth from his she rushed off.

Standing on the back balcony, Priscilla watched the sun dip lower and lower into the sea. Even removed as she was from the crowd and tavern, the rowdy laughter and lewd comments reached her ears. She focused on the lull of the sea as it connected to the land.

Off in the distance she could make out the sounds of the crashing waves as they collided with the rocky terrain found there. Each smash coincided with the shatters in her chest. She never felt so alone. Since she left Nathaniel and Lydia earlier, she remained absent. She didn't read with Alice.

It's not that she grieved for a friendship she never had. She just couldn't comprehend Lydia's motives.

"It's beautiful this time of day, isn't it? I haven't afforded myself an opportunity to recall it's magnificence in such a long time." Lydia approached behind her. Leaning her elbows on the banister, she gazed out over the sea. "You have avoided me all day. Not that I blame you. But I do owe you an explanation. You have been nothing but kind to me and especially to the children. You degraded yourself and co-conspired with Sabine allowing us the ability to stay here until Nathaniel's return. I am grateful."

Priscilla didn't acknowledge her, she had no response. She held her gaze straight out past the port.

Lydia continued, "I wasn't much older than Alice when we boarded the ship taking us from England. My father intended to teach our language and reading in the islands. Nathaniel's father planned to bring the word of God. Pirates attacked us. He and I hid in the pantry as instructed, but there is nowhere to hide when your ship is seized. They spared us... or so we thought. The only survivors. I'm sure he never told you, but when they unlatched the door and discovered us, Nathaniel went at them with a spoon."

Hearing this had Priscilla turn her head. Lydia had a slight smile, though her eyes revealed her suffering at retelling the horrific story. She sighed before resuming. "Yes. That is how he acquired the name. And the entire time I lived on that ship they never referred to him as any other name. They took everything from us. They were ruthless. They managed to steal his identity. If he corrected them and repeated his birth name, they whipped him."

How did Priscilla never question how he came to be a pirate? She assumed he chose that life. Hearing these details saddened her more. "I am sorry, Lydia. I didn't... didn't–,"

"We never talk of it. We never have. They worked him hard and endlessly. His hands bled and stayed infected. I cleaned and wrapped them the times they allowed him to come below and rest, but those times were short and rare. Neither of us knows the exact amount of time we sailed with them. Months at sea. Weeks in ports. Years passed. When they took leave of the ship, they chained me. I had no escape." Clearing her throat, Lydia twisted her head away from Priscilla's eyes. "Once Hackett began forcing himself on me, Nathaniel began talking and planning of how we might flee. By the time he had a strategy he felt comfortable with, I was heavy with child."

Priscilla never heard such a sordid and heart-rending story. Laying her hand over Lydia's she bit her lip to constrain the sobs.

Sniffling, Lydia faced her with teary eyes. "Nathaniel freed me. He brought me to Sabine. The two of them told Hackett when he discovered my absence, days after drinking and whoring at port, that Nathaniel brought me to Sabine after two days of difficult labor. They advised him that both the baby and I died. Sabine put herself at great risk for us. We will forever be in her debt." Stepping closer to the railing and stiffening her shoulders, Lydia cautioned, "Hackett need never learn that I survived and Henry is his son. He would certainly kill me and force Henry to the sea with him. I don't want that. I've never wanted that for him, but he is becoming a man. He should decide his path. I'm grateful I raised him away from that life... besides Nathaniel's influence. Nathaniel abided by my and Patrick's wishes and didn't speak much of his life away."

Priscilla hated to ask, but she wanted to know. "What about Patrick? Is he not at sea? He isn't a sailor?"

Lydia's jaw stiffened and her lower lip trembled. "He was an older gentleman, a farmer from Ireland. We met at market. He took me and Henry to his farm and we became a family. He lavished me with kindness and love. Together we had Alice, Joseph, and Hannah before the fever took him." Tugging her hand out from under Priscilla's, Lydia turned and pinned eyes filled with sadness and resignation on her. "So, depressing as much as all of this is, the reality is Nathaniel is a pirate. His heart is filled with vengeance and it belongs to the sea." Lydia walked off leaving her to replay the unimaginable in her mind.

The two of them endured tragedy together. And it continued for Lydia. She found happiness and lost it too. Lydia didn't need to expound on why she never corrected Priscilla's belief that they were married. Priscilla understood. If she didn't return to Charles Town, her life would consist of hardship and misfortune.

Empathy and indignity replaced the betrayal and astonishment of earlier. How could she have yielded to Nathaniel and all that occurred since they met? She accepted all he effected, not that she had much choice in the majority of the situations he forced her into, but why now did she still think she must do as he stipulated? She didn't.

For all her yearnings to be her own person and breakaway from rules and roles expected of her, why should she stray from that? If he intended to desert her, why follow along as a stray and starving dog willing to accept additional cruelty from an individual who mistreated it, just for a morsel of affection.

She and Sabine formed an alliance and entered into an agreement. Not Nathaniel. Their business would conclude when they decided. She didn't need his approval or his blessing. Seeking out Sabine, she did so not to defy him but to exercise her freedom and choice. Deliberating over Lydia's allegations and the validation beheld in Nathaniel's face, he had no loyalty to her. He proved it once already. He would leave her without any consideration or explanation.

Where she wanted to go and what she wanted to do, she didn't know. But she established she could make an income and whatever she decided would require payment.

Leaning her back and head into the door she closed connecting the two rooms, she sighed. The patron she and Cecile deceived smelled of ale and sweat. He became aggressive with her before she feigned modesty and met Cecile behind the screen to undress and leave the room. No candle burned and she found it odd as she intentionally left one going each night.

Shuffling to the side table to light one, a warm glow illuminated the space near the opposite side of the room. Nathaniel sat in the chair, his elbows on his knees. The hardness in his body and eyes worried her. Knowing eventually he and she would have this confrontation didn't prepare her for the actual occurrence.

"It's been a long day. I'm tired and wish to rest," she announced. To her relief, her words and deliverance sounded bolder and more determined than the beats of her racing heart in her ears.

Dropping his arms, he gripped a knee in each hand. His knuckles turned white with the clench he had on each one. "You are tired. You wish to rest, you say. Rather ironic that you admit this yet you chose to work tonight when I clearly told you not to." His golden eyes bored into her with such intensity she swore she saw flames dancing in them. A ticking in his jaw jiggled the earrings hanging from his lobes.

Noticing his damp hair pushed back behind his ears, she wondered if he bathed in this room while he waited on her. Not that it mattered where he did, but her mind conjured up images of his tan, taut body sitting in the tub she used.

Being in his presence incited strong responses in her body but left little else to steady and maintain a solid state of mind. His nearness tweaked all of her senses. Her fingers tingled longing to feel him. Her nose twitched yearning for his scent. Her eyes—she couldn't stop admiring him. Her mouth went dry parched for his taste. And his voice, no matter in anger or ecstasy, gave her the shivers.

"You have no reasonable explanation to provide me, Angel?" he inquired.

"I'm not obligated to provide you with anything. You left me here to fend for myself, and I have done so. If you will discard me sooner rather than later, I will do as I please. You promised me a return passage once we reached Tortuga, yet here I still am. I don't need you to fund it, I'll do it myself," she challenged.

The muscles in his arms and neck flexed. "Is that so? I didn't promise anything. I don't make promises. And I have not yet released you from my custody, so you are not able to make those presumptions. I will see to your care as I see fit,

Priscilla. And when you defy me and disregard my commands, you will be punished." He darted out of the chair towards her.

Leaping on the bed, she scurried to the other side. Making it to the door, she succeeded at cracking it open before his foot obstructed further progress. He slammed it shut with such force she worried it took off the tip of her nose.

Taking her with him, he returned to the chair he vacated. Tossing her across his lap, he lifted her dress and struck her quick and hard. She didn't care who heard, she screamed. She yelled as loud as she could.

But it became impossible to draw any air in once the pain registered. She bucked and kicked and hollered when she could manage to.

The door burst open and Jean-Paul's massive frame filled the space. Nathaniel stopped spanking her, but his palm held her firmly in place.

"Sorry for the intrusion, Master Davies. Madame Sabine requested I look in on Mademoiselle Belle as we heard her screams, and only she is expected to be in this room. *Bon soir*," he said backing out of the room and shutting the door behind him.

Her bottom burned and her face itched where tears rolled down her nose and cheeks. He didn't start up where he stopped, but he didn't release her either.

"Are you finished being mouthy and disobedient? That's twice I've had to punish you today," he asked. He presented the question as more of an understood statement. "Don't think I won't chain you up if I have to, Angel. Until such time that I give you leave of me, you are mine and I will not tolerate such insubordination."

"I'm not a member of your crew," she retorted.

The touch of his hand started to soothe her achy flesh. He caressed it, massaged it. "Come morning, you will board the 'Devil's Angel'," he announced.

The name of the vessel didn't go unheeded, but the mention of morning and her attendance took precedence. "What if I don't wish to leave with you?"

The softness in his touch stilled. The tips of his fingers kneaded her skin and grew deeper before he replied, "So now you don't wish to go with me. You seem incapable of deciding on what you want, Angel. More the reason why I must fulfill my duty of ensuring your safekeeping."

Folding her body over his legs, she arched her back swinging herself from his lap. Darting farther away from him, she derived a bit of bravery and confronted him. "I don't know what I want? Well I don't recall that being a concern of yours when you took me from the beach. I just informed you I don't need you to see to my return or to my journey anywhere."

He laughed. He laughed so hard his back collided with the chair. "Why must I repeat myself? I took you. You're mine. Until I say otherwise. Not that long ago you cried for me not to leave you. You have voiced your apparent dislike of any possible intention I may have of 'discarding' you. I have never indicated I have any notion of that. Undress and get in bed. Tomorrow we sail."

He made valid points and it irritated her. "I have a father. You dictating orders and spanking me like a small child is barbaric. And you laugh at me when I exercise my ability and right to make my own decisions."

"And a fine father you have. He allowed you to leave his safety with an unworthy chaperone. Perhaps he wanted to rid himself of you. Perhaps he decided you were too much trouble and he tired of the continual ache in his head you provided him." Rocking himself up and out of the chair, he glowered seeing her retreat and put more distance between them.

"My father is an honorable and respected man. He adores

me. He forbade me to travel to this uncivilized region, but I did so anyway without his knowing until we were far at sea. So, never ever speak of my father in such a manner again. I am certain you wouldn't take kindly to me speaking negatively about your father—." Forcing her lips together, she cringed over having mentioned his deceased father. Shock moved through his eyes before sadness settled in them.

Nathaniel raised his hands in surrender. "Yes, ma'am. So do you wish for me to return you to him then?"

Imagining the shame her recent actions would bring upon her family, she quickly replied, "No. I do not." She never expected to return, but she sealed her fate when she gave herself to Nathaniel. She could never go back. As criminal as his choice of trade and his oppression of her were during their short association, she witnessed and participated in occasions he expressed kind, heartfelt emotion.

Placing the toe of one boot on the heel of the other he removed it. Pivoting, he sat on the foot of the bed and took the other off. Pulling his shirt off over his head, he stuck his thumbs in his waistband and slid his pants off. Nude, his glorious body uncovered, he stretched back on the bed. His legs hung off the end. "Before I get comfortable, do I need to restrain you, or will you comply and allow us both to rest?"

Angling his head, he looked to her for confirmation. His hair hung down the side of his face trailing under his chin. The sting of her earlier words showed in his usually bright, sharp eyes. They appeared dull, defeated. The urge to crawl beside him, caress his face and soothe his woes consumed her. She hadn't meant to hurt him. Had she? She never considered herself insensitive or cruel before.

"I am sorry for mentioning your father," she offered. Refusing to act on her initial impulse, an apology seemed the best alternative.

If living among these people affected her character after a

couple months, she feared what she might become if she elected to stay. Nathaniel captured not just her, but her body and her heart. She realized heartache would become a constant. He was a pirate. She must maintain her practicality. "I won't be any additional burden. You may rest without any fear of me—"

Soft, steady snores interrupted her. Moving closer, he remained where he relaxed. Legs bent, his feet planted on the floor. With his mouth open and eyes closed, she noticed how much younger he appeared when his features were void of tension.

Ridding herself of her dress, she crept up on the bed pulling a light cover over her nakedness.

Chapter 9

A smack to her backside abruptly woke her. "Get up, sleepy Angel. Time to depart and return you to a more civilized lifestyle," Nathaniel announced.

On her stomach, she buried her face in the pillow. She didn't notice any sunshine peeking in through any crannies around the door, and her bruised bottom continued to send painful alerts to her foggy brain. "Where might this 'more civilized lifestyle' exist?" she muttered burrowing her forehead deeper into the feathered cushion.

"Just get out of bed and gather your things. Lydia and Alice saw to packing up what belongings were in their room. Henry transported those and them onboard already." He shook the bed jostling her around.

"All right. All right. I'm up." Flipping to her side, the cover fell from her breasts. Gripping it, she yanked it back up, but looking to Nathaniel, he saw them. Heat burned in his eyes. They stayed so fixated on her chest she glanced down to confirm she did indeed conceal them. "Will you turn around so I may dress?"

He did. He turned his back to her and marched across the

room. "If we didn't have to leave and weren't the last to board, I would remind you that I've gazed upon, feasted on, and possessed your exquisite form. Unfortunately, I can't afford the time to do so again at this moment." He groaned.

One advantage of living in the islands, dressing took a fraction of the time it did in society. Lacing up the bodice, she stepped into her shoes and asserted, "I am dressed now. Are you not going to tell me our plans? Are you returning me to Nassau, or do I get a say?"

Taking her hand in his, he guided her to the door. "You have no plans. I have plans and being that you are mine is all the information you require."

"I wish to give my farewells to Sabine. Can I be allowed to do so?" she requested.

"No," he answered.

"But that is rude. Lydia told me how she aided you in the past… and now she did so again. I can't leave on good conscience without doing so. Please," she pleaded.

Squeezing her hand tighter until she yelped, he hauled her into his solid chest. He glared down at her. "I said no. She has received my gratitude and been paid greatly for her assistance. I have more crucial tasks residing in my mind, so if you would so kindly stop chattering and allow me to get to the ship."

She struggled not to rebel and continue with her interrogations. Imagining another punishment on top of the newly formed bruising and throbbing in her bottom convinced her to refrain. The stench in the street and the multitude of drunken men sprawled on porches and in alleyways were her last impressions of Tortuga.

On the dock, she inhaled the odor of salt on the breeze. Once in the rowboat, relief she didn't expect developed and the scent of the sea soothed her.

Directed to go below with Lydia and the children while they prepared to sail, she did. Hannah and Joseph jumped

Nathaniel's Treasure

around and hugged her. They had never been on a ship. Alice didn't share their excitement, but she embraced Priscilla requesting her to sit with her. Noticing Lydia pacing the room Priscilla understood the uneasiness in Alice. One could only describe Lydia as detached and haunted. Her eyes were wide and vacant.

"I was told the books were brought onboard. Shall we find them and continue where we left off?" suggested Priscilla.

Alice nodded. The concern and uncertainty present in her young face pained Priscilla. She hoped whatever Nathaniel delivered them to, consisted of a life free of the dangers and tragedies Alice and Lydia experienced.

One couldn't ask for a better day to sail. Smaller than other ships he manned, the Devil's Angel embraced the winds and raced across the water. Prior to their departure Nathaniel informed the men and each signed Articles accepting the presence of the women and children and to not interact with them other than common courtesies and general exchanges.

This made Priscilla happy. She moved about the deck with Alice smiling and talking non-stop. It made him happy too. He enjoyed watching her and hearing her laughter. He expected being on a ship again would be difficult for Lydia, but he hoped she would find some peace before his course deviation and the onslaught began.

Midday on the second day, Lydia emerged. His chest ached observing the hardness and the suffering in a face still young and pretty. Odd, he contemplated, he would always view her as the young girl hidden with him in the pantry all those years ago.

He considered himself much older than his thirty-four years. It gave him consolation that he did remove Lydia from

99

Hackett and she found acceptance and adoration with Patrick for more years than she suffered with the ruthless pirate.

With the women onboard, it became abundantly obvious why they shouldn't be. Instead of concentrating on the tasks at hand, there he stood fretting over Lydia's mindset and the forthcoming temper she would let loose on him. And with Priscilla, he couldn't determine what objectives he had—if any. He wanted her. He took her. He had her. What now?

On the third day out, he decided to engage with them. He kept his distance, going as far as avoiding any interaction with any of them until that point. In all honesty, he wished to have created a positive on the verge of the negative. And after watching Priscilla and remembering her scent and her softness, he wanted more of it.

After tomorrow, he had to know what direction to take. Drop her in a port with the crew wishing to take leave or have her continue on to Barbados with Lydia and the children.

Standing behind Priscilla as she sat with Alice and the twins reading, he barely listened to the words. Her enthusiasm and drama she incorporated to the stories captivated even him. And he had heard the exact stories from the Bible as a young boy often.

Joseph loved learning about Noah's ark. He asked question after question about the different animals and he was curious as to why they didn't harm each other, as he had seen dogs and chickens fight.

Priscilla chuckled at most of his queries but provided explanations. At one point, she mentioned to Alice and looked up at him for reassurance, that perhaps, she chose the wrong passage to share.

Hannah started worrying that they were on a ship due to the same circumstances. She feared they would never see land again.

Intervening, Nathaniel proposed, "Hannah, sit still and listen. She isn't done yet. You don't know the ending."

Pouting, she plopped back down beside Priscilla. The conversation never ceased. They wanted to know more. They even fetched items for her to make drawings for them.

Lydia eventually joined them, and it pleased him more than he could remember to take time to enjoy each other and the beauty around them. He signaled for Henry to join them too. He earned a break. He worked hard and did his best to prove his ability and impress his worthiness of joining the crew. Henry took great pride in teaching the younger ones what he learned about the sea and sailing.

As the day ended and night set in, Nathaniel took his dinner in the unexceptional Captain's quarters with all of them. Even though the space provided enough area for a few to move about, with seven of them, it became loud and unnerving.

Lydia requested Henry take his brother and sisters to the small room next to them where she and the children slept each night and put them to bed. Without hesitation, Henry did as she asked. Immediately she turned her focus to Nathaniel. "What are we to expect tomorrow? All of this is just a diversion to what you intend," she accused.

"Are you the captain of this ship?" he growled.

She huffed before softening her tone and beseeching him. "Do not place my children in any of your schemes for retribution. I beg of you, Nathaniel. Do right by them, as you have me. I know you are torn. Torn between remnants of who you were and who you are destined to be. It is all in opposition to who you've become." She knelt by his chair and placed her hands on his knee. She gazed at him. "You don't have anything to prove... to any of us. We all can leave this behind us. And I won't allow Henry to be involved. I let him accompany you to retrieve the Intrepid, but I won't stand by idly and watch him become what you have. He, as we all do, deserves a life of peace... not hostilities." Receiving no response, she stomped out of the room.

It irritated him that not only did she discern his involvement with them that day as more than innocent enjoyment, but she confronted him in front of Priscilla. He had other plans for her, and he had no doubt she too would now interrogate him. Damn women. He didn't have the patience or the incentive to contend with any of it at that time.

Thumping his mug on the desk where they ate, he dictated, "Clean this up and get to bed. Wash up if you wish. I had water brought in earlier."

⁂

By Nathaniel's lack of argument to Lydia's claims, Priscilla knew this journey would not be void of conflict. Not that one could depend on that each time they left the presumed safety of a harbor, but if she understood correctly, he planned to seek it. She hoped and believed he would join her that night and sleep next to her... among other activities, but as the hours progressed, she concluded he would not.

Slipping on her night jacket, she went to find him. Sitting on deck with a couple other men drinking, he noticed her but continued conversing with the others, ignoring her. If they were to expect the next day to be a dreadful one, she didn't wish to be alone for the night.

Wrong or right. He brought her into that life—he would be the one to placate her when she required it. She didn't expect him to deny her. As she couldn't deny him.

"Nathaniel, come to bed," she insisted.

Persisting with his avoidance of her and joking with the crew, she almost repeated herself if not for the lift in his eyebrows. He heard her.

Walking closer and in between two of the men, she stood in front of him looking down at him. "I do not wish to sleep alone. Please join me," she requested, sternly.

Out of the corners of her eyes she glimpsed the heads of the two at her sides snap turning their focus to her. Irritation and shock emerged in Nathaniel's face. She feared he would take her over his knee then and there. Instead, he threw his head back and laughed. The others joined. She almost wished at that point he did grab her and shield her anger and embarrassment from them. Her face burned with both.

The impulse to run came strong. She felt certain, if nothing else, he wouldn't deny her an opportunity for sex. Tears threatened to come, but she fought them. Were they tears of fury or rejection? She didn't know.

"Any man would be a fool to turn you down, Angel," Nathaniel stated. Setting his cup down, he stood. "Don't indulge on the mead and rum all night, you scoundrels." Patting each of the men on the back, he placed a hand on her lower back and guided her away.

Approaching the steps leading below deck, he leaned in whispering in her ear, "You might be careful in the future what you request and how you do so."

A shiver ran up her back and across her shoulders. The bruising from her last punishment in Tortuga persisted. She imagined receiving new on top of the old could be more unpleasant and agonizing than the initial chastisement.

Shoving her inside the cabin, he entered and shut the door. "If you wish to voice your disapproval and question my decisions, don't. I have no patience or will for it. Absolutely none. I haven't served as quartermaster under two separate captains, earned the respect of fine crews, and command my own ship to have all of my authority challenged by a couple of women. I've had to make the hard judgments. I've had to execute them."

Pride. Nathaniel had it. He had it for what he endured, how he transcended, and what he would do. Lydia's lack of support and negativity dwelled on him. And Priscilla didn't suffer what they had, and she may not fully understand his motivations, but she did respect his dedication. Even if she disliked his ambitions, she could relate to feeling as if you could never experience true happiness and peace until you fulfilled them.

Taking his hands in hers, she moved as close as she could to him. Her chest against his. She kissed his chin. "I have no desire to talk tonight. But I do have desire."

The corners of his mouth turned up. His eyes found hers and the heat in them enflamed her fervent arousal to a degree it consumed her. A frenzy of hands and arms commenced. Hers in his hair, tugging his lips to hers. His under her thighs, lifting her to straddle his hips. Walking to the desk, he sat her on it. Baring her breasts, he placed his hand between them and guided her backward on the wood. He ran his tongue under each one, between them, and licked her nipples.

Arching her back, she yearned to touch him, but her arms were pinned to her sides by the night coat. He caressed her ankles and his hands traveled higher. Grazing her most sensitive spot, he continued to do so lightly with his fingertips until she bucked on the verge of begging him for more.

Inserting one finger inside her, he rubbed the top with his thumb. Her legs shook, and she moaned. Taking a nipple in his mouth, he sucked it. Hard.

Between the pulsation in her center and the torment in her breast, she dangled in a state of urgency and rapture. Thrusting his finger faster and deeper while teasing and skimming the sensitive spot above and torturing her breasts, she came. Rolling her head from side to side, she surrendered to the amazing sensations he induced in her.

So lost in them, she gasped when he entered her. Plunging

in completely. Raising her legs, he held them behind and under her knees and rammed into her. Over and over. This wasn't lovemaking. This was pure and primal lust. Watching him, watching her, they reached climax together.

Without hesitation, he lifted her from the desk and took her to the bed. He got in beside her, facing her. Sliding to her side, she admired him. And he her. Their breathing still escalated, they grinned and descended from their shared enjoyment.

Fearing whatever might occur the following day, she figured she needed to act on the opportunity to make her appeal. In all her indecisiveness since she met him, she couldn't ignore her true feelings. She gave herself to him on the Intrepid. All of herself.

Nothing else mattered in comparison to him. He chose her. Could that not mean a future in some form? She found something—someone that intrigued and inspired her unlike anything had before him. Why choose to let it go?

"Nathaniel…" she started.

Expelling a large puff of air that blew her hair back from her face, he reluctantly answered, "Yes?"

"So often you have mentioned I am yours. You must want me. Don't you want me to remain yours?"

The shine in his eyes didn't translate into aggravation, but relief? Could she be that hopeful?

"Why do you ask this? Do you want to?" he remarked. She heard an uncertainty and surprise in his voice.

"I do. Yes, I do," she answered definitively.

He grinned.

Her heart inflated with emotion so expansive she wondered if her body could contain it. Her throat swelled. She could barely swallow.

Reaching out, he rested his hand on the side of her face. "If I considered you a woman worthy of naming a ship after, you shouldn't have questioned the depth of my devotion. You are an intelligent woman." He kissed her tenderly. "You didn't comment when I told you her name, Devil's Angel. A ship encompasses all of me. The sea. My crews. And unfortunately, settling old scores. I can't promise you anything, Angel. I can't leave this behind and settle somewhere. My ghosts are still roaming these waters and I won't have them haunt me."

Closing her eyes, she nodded. The two of them never shared a true conversation, and the fact they were and one so honest and exposed made her happier than she had ever been. She could remind him that he delivered quite a punishment the evening he informed her of his choice of names, but she wouldn't risk disrupting their newfound intimacy. Biting her upper lip, she reopened her eyes. His golden ones warmed hers, and her heart. "You. That is enough."

His hand smoothed her hair back behind her ear and over her shoulder. His eyes remained on hers, suffused with pensive reflection. "I can't even promise that. I may not return."

"But you will want to? You will always plan to return to me?" She worried over how he may respond. What if she asked for more than he could or would ever give?

His grin returned, brightening his eyes. "That, I can promise." Leaning into her, he kissed her deep and soft. Rolling over her, their sweet kissing progressed into a slow, gratifying, rediscovery of one another.

Chapter 10

Tucked into Nathaniel's body, their limbs entwined, Priscilla rested better than she had since she didn't know when. Unfortunately, the banging on their door didn't quit. One would think when you don't receive a response from the other side the inhabitants don't wish to be disturbed.

Separating the hair at the back of her neck, Nathaniel planted soft, warm kisses there. The pounding at the door persisted. Cupping her breast, his lips roamed across her shoulder. Still, the knocking continued.

"Go away," he hollered. His hand slid from her breast moving lower.

The intruder pummeled the wood with both fists. "Open the door, Nathaniel. If you don't... I will admit myself," Lydia yelled.

"Whatever it is can wait. Of that I am certain," Nathaniel shouted.

The door flung open and Lydia stormed in. Pulling the cover up and over Priscilla, he spun around into a sitting position, his feet on the floor, and his glorious body on full display.

"You have no shame. At least cover your... your–." Lydia slung her arm in front of her eyes.

"I don't recall inviting you in. So whatever state you discover me in is of your own doing. Do you wish to leave now and we can revisit whatever issue you have at a later time?" he proposed.

"That island to our left, Saona, and the mainland on the right. What are you doing? I knew you weren't planning to go directly to Barbados. You are going to find the Spaniard? When will it ever end, Nathaniel? We can leave this behind. I don't want any more violence," Lydia pleaded.

Priscilla stayed as she lay. She didn't look at Lydia. She didn't say a word. Knowing something would occur, hearing what exactly, and learning of its proximity filled her with dread. Their talk of a future together could become just that —talk. Fear consumed her.

"You're a fool, Lydia, if you believed I would neglect retaliating against those that threaten women and harm children. You speak of it and berate me with your claims to know me. You remind me of my father and his character–," he thundered. "Any admirable man protects. And when he fails, seeks recovery and reprisal for any of his treasures. Human and tangible." Bounding off the bed, he lashed out at a chair with his foot. It crashed into the desk folding into a pile of broken wood. "I will no longer tolerate your outbursts, Lydia. I can have the men lower a rowboat down and you and whoever else chooses to... can row your merry asses to shore, take your chances with the Spaniards inhabiting this area, and wait for us to head back this way. Or you can keep your damn mouth closed."

Priscilla's body shot up off the bed at the start of Nathaniel's tirade. Switching her focus to Lydia, the tiny hairs on her neck and arms rose. If Lydia didn't stay, should she?

What had he done? Nothing he wouldn't do again. Nothing he couldn't rationalize. The quarrel with Lydia didn't weigh on him. He knew before he offered to have her taken ashore that she would stay. He didn't lie to Priscilla. The promise he made he could and would keep.

He would never stop wanting her. She embodied the myths of the 'sirens'. She bewitched him.

Sailing along the coastline, he felt comfortable with the women and children coming on deck. The Spaniards wouldn't be watching for them in that proximity. Their settlements would most likely be more inland hindering their ability to catch sight of the incoming threat.

Mid-morning they went by the island of Santa Catalina. Without any change in the weather, his calculations were perfect. They would anchor at dusk, locate the camp at dark, return to the ship by morning and proceed to Barbados unscathed. The pieces and the doubloons stolen from the farm would be in his possession. What the future held after, he didn't know. Executing the raid, returning to Devil's Angel, both of them, were his priority and focus.

The mood and morale between the crew and their additional passengers couldn't be any dissimilar. The men met first thing. Nathaniel ordered Priscilla, Lydia, and the children to go below while they convened. After their discussion, the men's enthusiasm for the upcoming assault transmitted in their songs and influx of activity above and below deck. The rigging—ropes, pulleys, sails all were examined. All guns and ammunition were inspected.

Lydia's mood corresponded with Priscilla's. Dread.

Anchoring in a section containing no evidence of any civilization, but near Santo Dominique, Nathaniel accompanied the boatswain and gunner below receiving their reports and examining their assessments. Summoning all back on deck, he conferred with the riggers and announced all appeared satisfactory. Addressing the men enlisted in implementing the land attack, they busied themselves with dropping the rowboats. The men staying onboard he instructed to remain there and keep alert.

The women and children received explicit demands to go below and not leave from there until they were under sail. Priscilla feared taking a breath. If she did, she feared she would fall apart. These feelings were the ones Lydia tried to spare her.

Could Priscilla live and love this way? She wanted to run to Nathaniel and beg him to stay. But she accepted this. She agreed to it. Had she known it would come so soon, would she have? If she had more time to love him, might it have been worse?

Pinching her lips with her teeth, she couldn't swallow. Her vision blurred with the tears she refused to let fall. She no longer deemed herself a strong woman. The discomfort in her chest provided a testimony of a disintegrating heart.

The pressure of a hand on her back caught her attention. Turning her misty focus to her side, she found Lydia. "Come with me. I know it hurts, but he doesn't need to see that right now. Everything is in perfect order. No captain could have done a better job. It's an excellent strategy and the ship is in great condition and well-equipped," advised Lydia.

"But I want to say good-bye," Priscilla muttered.

"No. No farewells. Bad luck. Come on." Lydia wrapped her arm around Priscilla's waist and led her away.

The twins were whiny. They cried wanting to get off the

ship and play on the beach. Priscilla sat by the porthole watching and waiting. Alice asked if she wanted her to read to her, but Priscilla declined. Surprisingly, Lydia sat with her and listened. Henry came and looked in on them periodically. He carved some figures and animals for the twins to keep them occupied. It did… for a little while.

Night came. Nathaniel did not. Besides her angst over Nathaniel's absence, the eerie silence on the boat unsettled her. Never had it been so noiseless. It gave the impression of impending doom. Made worse so, once Lydia had the children asleep in the next room.

Sitting with Priscilla, their hands clasped together between them in her lap, Lydia stammered, "I apologize for how I've treated you, and for all the things I should have said, and the things I should not have. I hope you can forgive me."

Prodding her gaze from the window, she peered at Lydia. She had no ill feelings toward her. But encapsulated in an essence of numbness she had no response, nothing to give her. Every fiber of her soul, mind, heart and body, were otherwise, occupied. She resumed her watch out the window.

"I knew when he brought you to the farm that you were special to him. I assume he has taken up with a whore a time or two, but he has never shown any genuine interest in a woman. Until you. I honestly wanted to protect you from resigning to a life of worry and waiting. He loves you. I see that. And I'm sorry. It is your decision… not mine. But I know from the time he rescued me from Hackett, everything he has done and strives to do is to ruin him or kill him, or I don't know," Lydia confided.

Lydia's assertions resonated with Priscilla. He loved her? She knew he cared for her, desired her, but love? She wished he did, otherwise she wouldn't have agreed to wait for him. And she didn't expect a declaration from him—yet.

Skeptical to admit her own heart, hearing another

witnessed it, and judging by the agony she currently existed in, she did love him. But could she love a man who pledged his heart elsewhere firstly? Could he ever love more than he hates?

"A man with ambition is proof he is capable of commitment," Priscilla asserted.

Through the darkness, she saw light. Didn't she? Edging closer, her nose to the window, she waited.

Again.

Bolting off the seat, her feet not quite under her, her elbow slammed onto the desktop preventing her from crashing into the floor. Lydia rushed to her side and reminded. "You know we can't go up. I won't allow you to."

"I have to know. I have to," Priscilla cried. All of the emotion she held at bay poured out of her. She trembled. She gasped. She sobbed. Shaking her arms at her sides in a feeble effort to rid herself of it, Lydia clamped her wrists over them containing them. Concentrating on Lydia, her soothing touch and calming words, Priscilla's wailing subsided into quick, soft huffs.

Wrapping Priscilla in her arms, Lydia rocked her. "Henry will come. He won't keep us waiting."

The two of them stayed in that position sharing and supporting each other long after the racket of activity sounded above them. Priscilla savored the comfort and companionship she acquired in that turbulent period of anxiousness. Her mother never hugged her. She never displayed any form of affection.

Hearing steps coming closer, they embraced each other tighter. The door opened and Henry appeared. "Nathaniel is safe. We lost four, but he requests you come above." Henry didn't say anything more, and it imparted a cryptic implication. Was Nathaniel wounded? He said safe, but did that denote unharmed?

She and Lydia followed Henry. The warm, night breeze gusted blowing her hair and skirt. As her eyes adjusted and she took in the scene, she surveyed the injured laid out. She observed members of the crew lifting items aboard. She didn't find Nathaniel.

"Is this him?" Nathaniel yelled from the left, far corner.

Straining to see him, joy overwhelmed her spotting him standing. Forcing the man he held in front of him forward, her joy turned to horror. The Spaniard.

Thick blood oozed and bubbled from his nostrils. One eye swollen shut and a wide gash above it at his eyebrow didn't diminish his arrogant and imposing attitude. He jerked to free himself of Nathaniel… to no avail. Lifting his chin, he sneered at her and rambled some words in Spanish she sensed were threats.

Lydia quickly responded to him, also in Spanish, before addressing Nathaniel. "Yes, Nathaniel. What do you intend to do? Didn't you get what you went for? Isn't that enough?"

The blade of the crude knife Nathaniel raised reflected the moonlight. Putting it at the Spaniard's earlobe, he jerked it down and across his neck. Priscilla shrieked dropping to her knees.

Blood sprayed over the deck. Nathaniel hauled him to the side and tossed him overboard. Wiping his hands across his shirt, over his abdomen, he ordered, "Clean the bastard's foul gore off my ship."

A couple younger crewmates started at it.

Priscilla vomited. She didn't have time to get up from her knees and make it to the railing. Closing her eyes, she refused to watch the blood thin and smear as they poured water over it.

"Have you gone mad, Nathaniel? Not only were you reckless, you're acting on impulse. How could you do that… in our presence? What a ghastly thing to do," condemned Lydia.

"How many of them are after you? You can't believe they won't search for him and seek you out?"

Nathaniel shouted out orders, little of which Priscilla heard, she knew they would sail shortly. Her head throbbed, and her continued heaving created aches in her stomach and chest.

"Take Priscilla below," demanded Nathaniel. "You know I wouldn't permit unnecessary killing. We retrieved what they stole, some additional goods for our journey, and I brought him back to make certain the correct man perished. Never again to harm another child."

Positioning her inner elbow and forearm under Priscilla's, Lydia assisted her to her feet. "We didn't have to bear witness to it. You chose that," she hissed.

After a day consisting of unbearable probabilities and heightened emotions shifting from one extreme to the other, fatigue set in. Priscilla didn't want to feel any longer.

Lydia untied Priscilla's bodice with shaking fingers. "I will remain in here with you. If you find that agreeable," she offered.

Her lips parted to speak, but no words came. Growing up as she had Priscilla never expected to see another human die. She had twice with Nathaniel. And they weren't deaths, they were murders.

Grabbing one of Lydia's hands, she held it between them, allowing her eyes to say what she couldn't manage. Lydia nodded. "Of course. Get in bed. I won't leave you."

Flattening her body to the wall, her forehead to the wood, Priscilla's mind and heart vaulted between resolutions. Learning more and more about Nathaniel and his way of life, would love be enough? Could her heart suffer and mend... suffer and mend?

How many partings and fears of him not returning could it tolerate until it depleted?

In spite of the adverse aspects, she loved him in ways she never dreamed possible. Could she deny her heart what it wanted?

Chapter 11

He acted on impulse. No refuting that glaring fact. And recently, he had been acting more and more on impulse. Why? Recalling the events since the day he took Priscilla, his devotion to pirating weakened.

Archer had been good to him. Taking him in well over a decade ago, a few years after he removed Lydia from Hackett's clutches. Archer sanctioned Nathaniel as a member of his crew and warned Hackett not to oppose him. And Nathaniel terminated their association with ingratitude and effrontery.

Not that he hadn't provided Archer with countless targets, complete with valuable cargo, but that didn't excuse his blatant disrespect of the captain and his Articles. The more he pondered it a startling revelation emerged. He didn't want to live that way any longer.

Hints of envy presented over the years. Watching Lydia find love and happiness. Interacting with the children. The moment he laid eyes on his Angel, his motivations and ambitions altered. She drove his compulsion to locate the Spaniard. No one would never terrorize her or threaten her again.

Little did it matter anymore. His actions validated Lydia's

contentions. A pirate through and through, he lived a life of danger and egotism.

Specks of salt struck his eyes, the sails flapped overhead, and he had a clearer image of his future. He beat Hackett when he stole Lydia and their unborn child, rescuing them from his malice. And that would suffice. The anger and defeat ensnaring him in an inescapable vise waned.

Since Priscilla, her exuberance, and her pursuit of living as she desired, he identified a concept so foreign to him—freedom. It wasn't his physical being enslaved all that time, freed when he went with Archer, but his heart and soul remained imprisoned.

Lydia and the children stepped on deck. Priscilla came next. She appeared tired, disenchanted and detached. She didn't engage with the children. She straggled behind them, expressionless. A tangled mess of white hair blew about her slender shoulders.

He broke her. His Angel. The bright light that clung to her like a halo, dimmed. Calling to his first mate, he set off to tell her of his change of heart, and his desire to stay with her wherever she wished to be.

A crack of lightning and a torrent of rain delayed him. How had he neglected to recognize the oncoming weather and its damaging potential? A rip in one of the sails lengthened.

Scanning the deck for a rigger, he glimpsed the silhouette of a ship up ahead. Broadside. Their current position, between the island of Saona and the mainland, he had minimal area to navigate. Shallow waters on either side. He must maintain a straight and forward course.

Why would a captain steer and hold that pattern against an unknown vessel?

The storm strengthened. The women and children went below. One less thing demanding his attention. The navigator hollered at him through the pelting downpour about the ship ahead. Nathaniel signaled his acknowledgement.

All the sails dropped by the riggers. They slowed, floating. But they couldn't keep Devil's Angel from running aground in the heavy winds. Surveying behind him, it came as no surprise to spot another ship, it too broadside. Trepidation took root in his soul.

This didn't strike him as a usual raid. Forethought and purpose went into this. Unlikely the culprits were the Spanish. They had a major lead on them. These offenders were lying in wait. He had no other choice but to anchor, trapping them between the two larger ships.

The twins were uncooperative and energetic. Lydia hoped to give them ample opportunity to run and play, but the storm struck quickly. They whined. They argued.

And Priscilla didn't know how much more she could take. She wanted to scream at them. Give them something to cry about. Exiting the confines of the cabin, she headed to the kitchen. Not that she knew what she might find to appease them, but at least she got the opportunity to flee the mayhem.

Unaware of much other than acquiring some silence, the man that lunged from around a corner blocking her retreat didn't register any warning. "Excuse me," she stated, attempting to squeeze by him.

His arm went around her clutching her neck. Hard. She squealed. He grasped her tighter. Her knees buckled, and he squeezed until her vision went gray. Hoisting her up and out on deck, she smashed face first on the soaked planks coasting and crashing with some barrels.

Catching her breath, she wiped her eyes. Many men she

didn't recognize stood about. A large man with a full, silver beard, held a pistol on Nathaniel. The stranger's eyes widened and a nasty, frightening leer crawled across his lower face. "Get her up. I thought I said don't harm anyone," he voiced to the man that hurled her out. Yanking a looped narrow strap from his belt, he gave it a strong shake, and it unfurled. Taking his arm behind him level with his waist, he swung it around to his front striking the man with the thin leather across his left ear and temple. The impact caused him to falter to one knee, but he quickly got back up. "Don't make me tell ya again. I won't be as gentle if ye force my hand," the intimidating man forewarned.

"Let her be, Hackett. She has nothing to do with this," stated Nathaniel.

Hackett? Complete terror seized her. Where did he and his men come from? The rain slackened, but still fell.

The man didn't lift her by her neck that time. He fisted her hair and snatched her to her feet.

"Now, Spoon. Do you believe you have any goods in your possession, including Miss Beale, I'm not entitled to? Pity you didn't gain any smarts after leaving my service." Rain droplets dribbled off his hat into his mouth and beard. Even so, nothing could diminish his menacing appearance and manner.

Beale? He said her name. How did he know of it? She hadn't shared that with anyone.

Hackett's mouth stretched open in a grotesque fashion and laughter burst from it. It subsided. It escalated. Looking to his men, she realized he wished for them to join him in his amusement. They did, but their eyes flitted to him and each other for validation.

"What is it, Miss Beale? You and Spoon expect to keep your little secret? Or perhaps, he failed to inform you of his knowledge and intention," he goaded.

No words came to her. Nathaniel's eyes came to hers, but he didn't speak either.

A struggle sounded along with Lydia's shriek of vexation. "I told you I would willingly come. Remove your hands from me. Now."

Hackett scared Priscilla before he laid eyes on Lydia. Noticing Lydia, he downright terrified her. His disbelief manifested for a brief moment before the comprehension of Lydia and Nathaniel's deception. Ferocity invaded him entirely, and Priscilla attempted to run to Lydia. Jerked backward by her hair, she yelped falling on her behind and dragged back to where she started.

"She's no good to either of us if you continue to mistreat her," roared Nathaniel.

Stiffening his arm with the barrel of his pistol pointed at Nathaniel's chest, Hackett threatened, "Don't you address me. If I return her minus a few bits, all the same. I'll still collect the ransom."

Ransom? Her father. Did Nathaniel know of it? Did he not plan to take her on to Barbados?

"Come to me, Lydia. You look lovely for a woman dead for eighteen years." Hackett tilted his head, scrutinizing her. "Very well indeed. Out of all my whores, you were one I thought about in your absence. Once, maybe twice."

"Don't call her a whore! She is a fine woman. A great mother and wife." Henry came up behind Lydia taking position in front of her.

Striding closer to Henry, Hackett studied him. "I can't be certain. I don't necessarily see a resemblance. But I assume you are my deceased child." Swinging the pistol off of Nathaniel, he aimed it at Henry and fired. "And now you truly are."

Henry's body convulsed. His arms launched out and back guarding Lydia before he crumpled to the ground.

Lydia screamed, throwing herself over Henry. Nathaniel rushed Hackett but failed to reach him. Four men charged him. They wrestled him to the deck and commenced beating him with short clubs and kicking him unrelentingly.

Nathaniel's horror ridden eyes stayed on her until the beating became too much and they fluttered closed. The men continued their assault. The image of his limp, bloody body and Lydia's wails obliterated all she thought she knew and ever wanted to know. Gone were her dreams. Her immature fancies.

She acted without fear, without hesitation. Clutching the top of her bodice, she ripped it open. At the waist where her skirt joined it, she tore out the folded gully given to her by Sabine and sewn into her gown. Knowing she had it available did provide comfort while she worked and encountered belligerent sailors. She never expected to use it.

Prying it open, she darted at Hackett. Leaping onto him, his back to her amidst hailing their triumphs of capturing the Devil's Angel and trouncing its captain with his crew, she plunged the blade in the side of his neck. He bucked and spun across the deck attempting to dislodge her. Extracting it, she stabbed him again at the front of his neck.

Blood pumped out of the slashes, impairing her vision, but she held tight and knifed him repeatedly. He stumbled several times. Slipping on the deck wet from rain and blood. Yelling obscenities, he fell to one knee. Bounding upright, his body tipped. Falling backward, her underneath him, her head contacted the railing. It cracked with the impact and the weight of her and Hackett's bodies.

Every portion of his body protested during his parade of prestige. The sun shone brightly and the men paused for him in respect and allegiance. He dreamed of that day, but his spirit perished. The trauma to his exterior would heal. His soul would not.

He... Priscilla defeated, killed Hackett. With his death, Nathaniel had a combined crew numbering over a hundred men and a fleet consisting of three ships. And it meant nothing to him. He listened to Lydia's mourning through the walls while he mended.

All the occasions he yearned to call out to her, he never did. Henry died defending his mother's honor. Nathaniel prayed his demise befell him prior to him perceiving it occurred at the hand of his birth father.

If Nathaniel didn't have plenty to loathe, him shouldering the bulk of the blame, the surgeon explained to him that Priscilla may never wake up. Even if she managed to, she would be damaged. If she regained any memory, she could have diminished mental capacity.

What did that mean? What was the doctor telling him? Should he and the others have left her in the shallow waters where she sank? All the doctor provided him with were speculations. Did he deduce letting her die to be more merciful than attempting to save her?

He still held hope.

Straining to see anything through the blood and swelling, he watched her fall over and into the sea with Hackett. Managing to lift his arm in that direction and gurgle her name, men scattered to retrieve her. He saw them place her limp body on deck and pump and beat her chest until they established a pulse.

Demanding the men to leave him as he lay for the first two nights, he allowed them to assist him to the cabin where she rested on the third day. And rested. No sound. No movement. Except the rise and fall of her chest. He sat and slept in the chair. He couldn't bring himself to disturb the healing she required.

The howls of anguish behind the wall from Lydia compounded his misery. He issued no orders to set sail. Where to? For what? He went through the events over and over in his mind. Wishing they produced a different outcome.

"Nathaniel, it's been a week. I don't blame you. I can't. If you didn't come look on me that day eighteen years ago and taken me to Sabine, Henry may have never been born. If I too didn't survive, I wouldn't have met Patrick. I wouldn't ever have had the chance to love Alice, Hannah and Joseph either. And I don't regret a single moment I had with Henry. He brought laughter... lots of laughter. Quite the jester. Responsible when necessary. And I'm thankful I shared what I did with him. I love you. And you love me. We have relied on one another for a long time. And I'm so, so sorry for faulting you for your goals, no matter how bewildering they were to me—they were yours. And they didn't cost me my son. Too many blames to place on one man. I can't. You never harmed me. You didn't kill my Patrick or burn my farm. You've done so very good by us. Do it for her," pleaded Lydia. She stood in front of the desk across from him, but he couldn't look at her. His eyes went and stayed at the floor.

Lydia raised her voice. "Nathaniel, don't ignore me. Return her to her father. If what Hackett said is correct, he's looking for her. Perhaps he can find a more experienced doctor. You have a crew of men to manage. A great number of them. If you don't resupply they will become unruly, dangerous. I'm sorry, I truly am, but for someone who achieved what they set out to... you're behaving as a coward.

Priscilla loved you. Be the man deserving of that love. Be him now."

Priscilla. His temper breathed. A beast he didn't recognize or know if he could control. Leaping off the chair and over the desk, he caught Lydia around the throat. "Don't…" Every emotion raging inside him stared back at him through her eyes. He let go of her. "Always the voice of reason, Lydia. I will see to it."

Dropping back into the chair, he looked over at Priscilla. She still looked angelic, peaceful. She gave him what no one and nothing else could, unconditional adoration. His first sight of her, he coveted her as he had no prize before. Stealing her was worth any costs to him.

She wanted him as he wanted her. She chose him after all he forced on her. She viewed him as he always wanted to view himself. And coming from such a magnificent treasure as she, he vowed to cherish her and do anything in his power to keep her. Keep her safe. He failed. Did he expect a different outcome? No man, especially a pirate would be worthy of her.

Chapter 12

The aches in her head rarely subsided. And the loss of hearing in her right ear fostered her flawed and contaminated opinion of herself. Her father coaxed her out on deck each day for a stroll and she sensed the eyes of the crew appraising her.

An officer's daughter taken and subsisting with bandits. Their imaginations conjuring deviant scenarios. And now returning as an impaired and undesirable woman.

She heard their whispers.

"Priscilla," her father called from outside the door. "We've arrived. Your mother will greet us. Let's not keep her waiting." He paused. Chances were he hated those two associations as much as she—mother, waiting. "When you are ready. I'll be here outside the door."

Her thoughts went to Lydia. What happened to Lydia? She continued to struggle with her memory. Her father had been patient and comforting with her. He didn't question her, but he didn't provide any answers either. Supposedly, Nathaniel delivered her to him in Nassau. She assumed after receiving the ransom, he departed.

Regaining consciousness two days prior to find herself with her father and on a ship headed away from the islands came as such disorientation the doctor had mildly sedated her. Her father informed her they left for Charles Town as soon as he had her safe in his care and the doctor deemed her worthy of sea travel.

Blood and murders plagued her whether awake or asleep. The trembling would start and her chest compressed. She mumbled verses refusing to surrender to the revulsion and the torment. Fearing if she allowed it to leach further in her soul, it would consume her.

Everything changed, but now it seemed the time had come for her to resume her initial path laid out for her by her mother. She wondered if the heart beating in her chest would ever pound for anything or anyone other than simply sustaining her life.

Nathaniel left her. He discarded her when he believed she no longer had worth. He promised her he would always want her and return to her.

The debilitating headaches encumbered her thought process. How long had she been in a comatose state? Days? Weeks? She hadn't asked. Concepts entered her mind and disappeared quickly.

Joining her father, he escorted her from the ship and onto land once again. Walking the distance of the pier exhausted her. He tucked his arm into hers supporting her. Pointing to a carriage off to the left with his free hand, he stated, "There it is. We're almost there."

Abraham, one of the servants her mother insisted on keeping, waited to assist her inside. She smiled at him. He returned it with a shy grin, lowering his eyes. Priscilla liked the way Lydia and the individuals she interacted with while away related to the coloreds. Not that she, herself, ever degraded the ones in their household, but she vowed to associate with them more from there on.

Taking the seat across from her mother, the inspection began. "Oh how dismaying. You look absolutely appalling," her mother complained.

"Cornelia, that's a fine way to greet your daughter," her father scolded.

Pursing her lips, her disdain evident, she continued, "Am I not correct, Lemuel? One would expect darkened, dry skin from gallivanting around under the island sun. She is the complete opposite. Pale, sickly. There's no shine to her hair. Has she even handled a brush?"

Priscilla closed her eyes. The energy and inclination to bicker with her mother as she always had in the past eluded her. She wanted a bed. Her head hurt and she was fatigued. Anticipating going from the carriage to her room greatly appealed to her, but it required energy she worried she couldn't muster.

"We will discuss this once we are home, but I am grateful to have her back and alive." He took Priscilla's hand in his and placed them in his lap.

Thankfully, her mother remained quiet the rest of the journey. Priscilla sensed her studying her and her aversion mounting. Not that she ever had any adoration for her only child.

The next month proved to be slow and excruciating. Keeping to her room and to herself forced Priscilla to confront the realities. Nathaniel was gone. Lydia and the children were no longer a part of her daily life. Henry died.

And she jabbed a blade into another human being killing him. The tears came. She wailed. Would it ever end? Every piece of her hurt. Breathing pained her.

As broken as she existed, she couldn't control the crying

spells when they surfaced. One afternoon sitting outside, it started. The harder she attempted to suppress it the fiercer it came. Sobbing until she gasped for breath, Coffey, one of the house-servants, came for her and took her to her room.

Priscilla and her mother saw each other at the evening meals. Those included grimaces and snide remarks until Priscilla excused herself. Father had been home the first two weeks but had to leave after that.

Declining dinner the night of her breakdown, her mother knocked on her door and entered. "I think it's time all this pathetic sulking ends. You can blame your father for encouraging you to act on wild impulses. He indulged your imagination and promoted you swaying from a woman's conventional course."

"I don't fault him. I never have need to wonder what more is out there." Priscilla stifled a sob. She knew what was out there—Nathaniel. Maybe it would have been best to never have known him. Sitting in her reading chair, the same book she opened weeks ago still on the first page in her lap, she didn't look up and acknowledge her mother. "If Father didn't influence me as he had, I wonder if I would still be alive. I encountered and experienced situations that surely would have defeated you."

Her mother's loud huff grabbed her attention. Lifting her head, Priscilla met her empty eyes with challenging ones. Her mother voiced one notable allegation—the time had come for pathetic sulking to end.

Pining for what could have been didn't help her in the 'now'. Not allowing her mother to belittle her and slight her would best benefit her. That hadn't changed. Recouping her fortitude and conviction became her priority. She hadn't been herself, and she would never be if she didn't make a start.

"So, Mother, I assume you have some suggestions you would like to… offer," taunted Priscilla.

Snapping her shoulders and back rigidly, her mother's face pinched so tight it appeared downright uncomfortable. She admitted, "Well, I do actually. Fortunately, Gideon has remained unmarried. He is willing to have you as his wife. I have a seamstress arriving in the morning to fit you for a gown. When your father returns, we will have the wedding."

Priscilla's mouth parted to relay her objections, but she paused considering the idea. She enjoyed Gideon's company. Possibly involving herself in another relationship might alleviate the demise of the other one. And it would get her out from under her mother. "I agree. Let's begin preparations."

Stumbling backward a step, her mother's eyes widened as if she took a direct pistol shot. She stammered, "Oh... oh, marvelous. Marvelous. Would you like a warm bath? I can have Coffey carry up some heated water and pour you one?"

Shaking her head in disbelief, Priscilla couldn't help but grin. She couldn't recall a time her mother ever asked if she wanted for anything. "No. I'm happy sitting and reading. Good night.

On the outside, Priscilla probably seemed 'normal', for her anyway. Her boldness returned. Her health returned. Not her hearing in the one ear, but it improved a little. It could be worse. She gained some weight back and painted a false smile across her face when in the presence of others.

At night, she buried her face in her pillow screaming and crying. Why did she continue to suffer in Nathaniel's absence? Did she truly expect to live out her life on an island somewhere as his?

Gideon visited with her often during the weeks before the wedding while they waited on her father to return. As dashing and immodest as always, he would never be faithful to one woman. She always knew that, and never intending to marry him in the past, it didn't disturb her. It still didn't.

"Priscilla, we need to discuss something. And I don't want you to misinterpret my intentions. I am very fond of you. You are breathtaking, in beauty and spirit. I sense your indifference to our union. And though we will present a splendid and enviable couple, this marriage can be what you wish it to be. If that is in name only, I will have no expectations exceeding that." His warm, kind, flirtatious brown eyes took on an earnest appeal.

She chuckled. "Are you trying to apprise me of your clandestine tendencies? I have witnessed you with numerous women over the years, Gideon. Your reputation precedes you throughout the colonies, not just Charles Town."

Grinning at her, he continued, "And being the astute woman you are, I believe you don't expect anything different from me. I understand you only agreed to marry before you left because you required my assistance in gaining access to the ship. Your father confided in me after your return that your heart belonged to another."

Hearing this stunned her. True, she and her father spoke nothing of what transpired during her absence or the contact he had with Nathaniel. He left before she regained the mentality to discuss it. Judging by the lump in her throat and the quivering of her bottom lip, she doubted her capability of doing so still.

It entered her mind to question her father about the proceedings surrounding his recovery of her, but her apprehension kept her from doing so. Did Nathaniel deliver her? Take the payment? Leave and never think of her since? How did her father know she loved her captor? Exactly what relation did he believe she had with Nathaniel?

Threading his fingers through hers, Gideon lowered his head, his eyes finding hers. "I upset you. The very thing I wished to avoid. I wanted to be honest and... blunt so to speak. As I knew, you would appreciate it and better identify with it if you understood this will be whatever form of a marriage you desire. I thought if you learned I didn't expect you to consummate it, you would feel less anxious about it."

"Have I appeared anxious to you?" she challenged. The 'marriage' didn't cause her anxiety. Nathaniel did.

Nodding, he smiled. "No, no you have not. And if you desire a marriage true in nature, I will be the faithful husband you deserve. And if you choose not to, I will practice discretion if I ever..." They bumped heads doubling over in laughter at his declaration.

Leaning in, she pressed her forehead to his. "How about we take our time and see what might develop. Having experienced..." she began. "Be assured, I understand the allure of a physical relationship.

***

"Stop shrugging and shifting. You are behaving worse than when I dress Joseph," scolded Lydia.

Nathaniel grumbled. "Since when has he ever had to wear this constrictive, impractical clothing."

Had all common sense abandoned him? It did the day he stole his most valuable treasure. He sighed. Lydia didn't deserve his impatience. For a man that weathered dangerous storms at sea, risked his life during numerous attacks and battled countless times, he currently experienced nervousness unlike any before.

Did she hate him? Did she ever love him? Could she still love him? What if she did both? Which one would prevail, love or hate? He couldn't live another single day without knowing—without seeing her, without trying.

Slapping Coffey's hands away from her head, she stamped her foot and slapped her hands on her hips. "What the hell is going on? Why did we come here? Mother doesn't want to bear witness to her unmanageable daughter getting married?" Priscilla shrieked. "She orchestrated all of this, and now she wants no part of it?"

She and Coffey forged a friendship and the gentle woman tilted her head, scrunched her lips and resumed arranging Priscilla's hair.

Swatting Coffey away again, Priscilla went and sat in the chair. Her father came home the prior evening. They shared dinner discussing the nuptial taking place the next morning, and her parents dismissed her to her room. She heard them arguing. For as long as she could remember she heard her mother's nagging and griping in raised voices, but not until that night did she ever hear her father elevate his.

Eventually she fell asleep. Coffey woke her and ushered her up and out of the house. A carriage waited out front. It took them to a couple's home, acquaintances of her father's, individuals her mother chose not to associate with. For whatever reason.

No one appeared to be home, but a servant gave them entry. Her wedding dress and her other essentials waited on her in a downstairs room. No one had come since they came. She dressed. Coffey did her hair. The minutes went by. "Can you go ask the man that let us in when we can expect someone? My father? Gideon?" Priscilla urged.

"Yes, ma'am," Coffey replied.

Too long ago. Coffey left almost an hour ago. What did it all mean?

Did Gideon decide he didn't want to marry? Or did he

decide he didn't want to marry her? Was her mother so beside herself she chose to extricate herself completely?

Priscilla folded her hands in her lap and stared out at the leaves falling from the tree with the drizzle and wind. She wondered what kind of weather Lydia might be experiencing. But she knew the answer. Sunny. Hot.

And she berated herself, speaking aloud, for switching her focal person from Nathaniel to Lydia. She couldn't lie to herself and believe she was healing because she substituted Lydia into her musings instead of Nathaniel. Yes, she cared and thought of Lydia nonstop. But why continue lying to herself about what she truly wanted. He never left her mind, her soul, her heart. Every living, breathing, remaining fragment of her yearned for him.

She couldn't do this. She couldn't vow something she no longer possessed. Living another day with uncertainty delivered a future of bleakness. Each day a little of her would die. Who would choose a slow death? Even if she never found him, or he rejected her, she belonged somewhere other than there.

She tried. She tried to forget about life outside of Charles Town. A life without Nathaniel. But she couldn't.

Rushing toward the door to locate her father and get much needed answers, it opened. Doing her best not to collide with neither, the door or the person, her nose pressed into a new, stiff cravat. Rushing her words to release them before anyone tried to reason with her, she blurted, "Father, I can't do this. I don't want to marry Gideon. I want to return to–" Tipping her head back, she gazed into familiar, warm, golden eyes.

Grinning, Nathaniel requested, "Continue, please. You wish to return to–"

Stepping away from him, she froze. Her heart beat as if it would burst from her chest. He wore stockings, breeches, a vest and a hat. She never gazed upon a more handsome gentleman. She wanted to jump in his arms, kiss him all over, remove all his fine garments… she wanted so much and did nothing.

"Are you not going to finish your statement?" he pressed. The glint in his stare confirmed he knew exactly what she intended to state.

"What are you doing here? I figured you'd be off sailing the oceans doing what you love more than anything or anyone," she barked, and instantly regretted. She watched his fingers stiffen in his right hand before relaxing once again.

His laughter echoed in the room. "Even when you are most likely still in somewhat of a delicate condition you wish to tempt me into punishing you. Not today, Angel." He strutted inside the room, closer to her. She retreated as he advanced. "I'm here for you. You are what I love… more than anything, more than anyone."

She swore her heart stopped pumping before resuming harder and quicker. How did he know where to find her? Did he realize it was her wedding day?

"How? Why? You left me. You gave me back," she accused. Counter arguments against surrendering to what she desperately wanted raced through her mind. "You did it for the ransom? Was Hackett right? You knew about it. Did you ever intend to take me with you?"

"From the first time I saw you, I intended to take you. And I did." Removing his hat, he tossed it on the bed. His brown hair brushed off his face and tied behind his neck provided a clearer view of the gold earrings hanging from his ears.

Tears filled her eyes, but instead of all the ones she cried in agony, these were blissful. He came back for her. He risked sailing to Charles Town. He bought and dressed as a nobleman, minus the jewelry, which he must have overlooked. And she found it incredibly charming.

But could she endure another heartbreak?

"Priscilla, look at me," he commanded. She did. "I never wanted to leave you. After the events that day, losing Henry, seeing you… as you were. Lydia encouraged me to take you to your father in the hopes he could attain appropriate treatment for you. It was the most difficult decision I ever made."

She mumbled, "You did it for the ransom."

"I did not," he denied. "I never knew of it until Hackett mentioned it. And I didn't accept it."

Did he speak the truth? "I can verify that with my father, you realize," she challenged.

"And I hope you do. Lemuel is a fine man. Your opinions of him were accurate. I have great admiration for him." His eyes pleaded with her. She knew he spoke the truth. His gaze exhibited hesitation and optimism. And it promised devotion and enthusiasm.

But could she survive losing him, again. Her opposing emotions overwhelmed her. A single tear slipped from one eye.

Kneeling on one knee, Nathaniel reached out a hand to her. "Priscilla, be my wife. I will do anything in my power to ensure you cry only happy tears for the rest of your life."

She never wanted anything so much. And she never would again. But it scared her. Shaking her head, the tears flowed. "I can't do it. I can't stay behind and wait and wonder. It hurts too much," she sobbed.

Dipping his head, he sighed. Lifting it, he demanded, "Come here." He patted his knee for her to sit.

If she did as he wanted, would her resolve crumble? She felt positive it would. "I can't… please, Nathaniel. I can't," she cried.

He slapped his thigh. The crack caused her to jump. "Woman… I have remained in contact with Lemuel receiving accounts of your condition, physically and mentally. I dressed in these preposterous garments. Professed my love. Promised to do what I can to keep you happy. What more is it you desire? Perhaps it isn't me. Was I incorrect, as was Lemuel, in that you return my feelings?"

"I can't have you leave me again. If your heart belongs to your ship and the sea and pirating, before me, I will be secondary to those. I won't live my life partially fulfilled."

Lunging at her, Nathaniel hauled her to him. She twisted and pulled, crying, "Please don't. I don't want to be spanked. I can't suffer anymore."

Arranging her on his bent leg, he wrapped his arm around her holding her to him. His warm, soft lips pressed to her forehead. He kissed her tears. Her nose. Placing them on her lips, he held them there. She continued crying. A soft, silent sobbing.

He spoke into her lips. "I no longer need to search for anything. I found a treasure worth keeping. Your father arranged a pardon for me. We can take up residence in the colonies or sail to Barbados. It is your choice, Angel."

Her lips bounced onto his. Her body racked with her weeping. Joyful weeping.

Alice hollered from inside the house. "Priscilla. Where are you? We've missed you."

Touching Nathaniel's face with her hands, Priscilla caressed it. "You are all here?" she giggled.

Laying his forehead on hers, he consoled, "Yes, we are all here. Seems we all want to keep you. If, you will let us?"

Lurching to go and greet the others, Nathaniel caught her forcing her back on his knee. "I, as well as your father, who defied your mother and arranged all of this, deserve an answer. Do we not?"

An answer? Overcome with all of it, she gazed into his mesmerizing eyes searching for guidance. Did he wish to know where they would live? She figured consulting with Lydia on that decision would be considerate if it involved all of them.

"Will you be my wife, Angel?" he repeated.

Throwing her arms around his neck, she hugged him as hard and as close as she could. "Yes!"

Epilogue

Hearing Priscilla pledge her life and love to him were the happiest moments of his life. If only he deserved her love. If only he could have stayed away from her. But he loved her. And no matter what transpired from that day forward—he would protect her and profess his love to her until his dying breath.

The small service consisted of himself and Priscilla, of course. Along with Gideon, Lydia and the kids, Lemuel, Coffey, and the preacher. Nathaniel prayed Priscilla chose to leave the colonies. If she did not, he would be forced to manipulate her. He didn't want to.

Recruiting Lydia to aid in his endeavor seemed like a detrimental option. Staying in the colonies, having the children attend school, and staying as far away from the danger and tragic memories of a pirate's life were her preferences.

Before the wedding he had not met Gideon. Though he and Gideon would be connected from that day on for an indeterminate amount of time. Lemuel was a loyal officer and staunch advocate for English rule. And he ensured any man desiring to be a member of his family and marry his daughter share his principles.

Lydia had no knowledge of the stipulations in the mediations between Nathaniel and Lemuel, and later with Gideon. Nathaniel thought he had reservations about the two men before that day. Now he realized he severely underestimated their shrewdness. Witnessing Gideon overtly flirting with Lydia twisted his stomach. The suspicion of what Nathaniel believed a seemingly harmless agreement began appearing more and more as if he made a deal with the devil.

"Father says we are staying here this evening. Including Lydia and the children. We have limited time before we decide where we go from here." Her cheeks were flushed. He couldn't believe this perfect angel agreed to be his wife. He worried about her becoming overexcited. Last time he saw her he didn't know if she would ever wake again. "I know. I am being impatient. I know once my mother receives word of my marrying you and not Gideon…" She breathed deep and sat in a nearby chair.

"You do not answer to your mother any longer. Only me." He grinned at her and rolled his eyes. As if. "Let us enjoy and celebrate our day. I want you to relax. Your mind and heart. I am here. I am with you always."

An uneasiness came over him. He noticed Lemuel walking in his direction. But he sensed something else caused his disquiet. Surveying the room, he glimpsed Alice. She smiled when their eyes met. But he received a bad, distinct feeling she comprehended much more than she should. He stepped away from Priscilla and out of hearing distance before her father reached him.

Lemuel stood beside him. He brushed his shoulder with Nathaniel's and muttered, "I received news and it is expediting I secure my interests in the future of Nassau."

Nathaniel did not give a damn about Lemuel and his

interests, except for Priscilla. Of course, that was easier said than done. If she had not been critically injured and he never had to seek out her father—they could be in Barbados living a life free of others and their selfish motives.

"Not tonight. It is my and Priscilla's wedding night," Nathaniel snapped.

Stiffening, Lemuel warned, "I will take my leave now. In the morning I expect to learn of you and your new bride's desire to return to the islands. Under the flag of the crown. And with Gideon."

Barely regaining his composure as Lemuel went to give his farewells to Priscilla, Lydia rushed over to him. "I have yet to discuss it with Priscilla and I do desire to consider her wishes, but Gideon is leaving the day after tomorrow for Nassau. If we decide to leave the colonies for Barbados, this would be the safest method. Sail under the protection of the Royal Navy. And I feel confident Gideon would accommodate us."

Separating himself from everyone and freeing his mind of anything except Priscilla were his priorities for the evening. Gideon influenced Lydia to modify her objectives in a matter of hours. It disgusted him. Once they arrived in Nassau, they would not leave for Barbados. Not without him becoming a fugitive. A traitor to the crown sailing the seas with the navy on his tail and the threat of encountering Archer once again.

Nathaniel entered an agreement, one in which if he ever wished to be free of, could cost him the very thing he did it for. His Angel. His treasure. Priscilla.

For her, he will do what he must.

Taking Priscilla's hand, he drew her out of the chair and into his arms. He gave her a quick, sweet kiss on her perfect mouth. "It is time for you to retire for the evening with your husband. I cannot risk having you fatigued from all the day's events and visiting with everyone." Her blue eyes widened. Nuzzling her neck, he kissed her earlobe and whispered, "I am anxious to claim my bride in the most intimate and salacious of ways."

Her jaw went slack, and he heard her barely audible pants of eagerness. He nipped her ear before repeating, "I love you, Angel."

The End

Sheri Lynn

Sheri Lynn was an Army brat, so her childhood involved moving every three years. However, truly a southern gal, she currently resides in Alabama with her husband, two Chihuahuas, a mean cat, turtle, and a teenage daughter. She also has two sons, who live on their own, and a stepson and stepdaughter.

Romance novels have always been her reading choice. She is a hopeless romantic, and that trait materializes in every aspect of her life. "Wearing your heart on your sleeve" has been a common phrase repeatedly heard in her life. Writing romance and 'happily ever after's comes naturally.

Whether a result of her childhood or not, she loves to travel. Warm weather and beautiful beaches are always her choice destination.

Don't miss these exciting titles from Blushing Books and Sheri Lynn!

The Heart Facts
The Heart Won't Forget, Book 1
The Heart Will Lead, Book 2

Heroines of Neoma Series
Charm Him, Disarm Him, Book 1

Eternal Gifts Series
His Eternal Promise, Book 1

Anthologies
12 Naughty Days of Christmas 2016

Contact Sheri Lynn:
sherilynnauthor@yahoo.com

Blushing Books

Blushing Books is one of the oldest eBook publishers on the web. We've been running websites that publish spanking and BDSM related romance and erotica since 1999, and we have been selling eBooks since 2003. We hope you'll check out our hundreds of offerings at http://www.blushingbooks.com.

Blushing Books Newsletter

Please join the Blushing Books newsletter
to receive updates & special promotional offers.
You can also join by using your mobile phone:
Just text **BLUSHING** to 22828.